Cast of Characters

Pat Abbott. A lanky San Francisco private eye, recently discharged from the Marines. He looks a little like Gary Cooper.

Jean Abbott. His wife, she met him in New Mexico. She does little detective work herself but is a keen observer.

Sam Brandish. A San Francisco police inspector who knows Pat all too well.

Ernest K. Leland. The first victim. He's rich and successful, age 40.

Nancy Moore Leland. His much younger estranged wife and friend to the Abbotts.

Rufus Moore. Nancy's older brother, he works for Ernest

Helen Moore. Wife to Rufus, she was once an aspiring actress known as Elaine Bishop.

Gwendolyn Telfer. With an assist from Ernest, she's made it big in advertising at age 27. She claims to have Nancy's interests at heart but her heart really belongs to

Philip Hannegan. A wounded veteran, he's in love with Nancy, not Gwen.

Chris Leland. Ernest's 17-year-old son from his first marriage. He's a college dropout with a major grudge against his father.

Mary Wang. Nancy's hard-working cook and housekeeper who is putting seven daughters through college.

Rosalie Wang. One of Mary's daughters, she works as a maid for Nancy but is also a sophomore in college.

Madame Madeleine. At Gwen's request, she made a shocking pink hat for Nancy which could just send her to the gas chamber.

Marco Jones. A waiter at a Mexican restaurant.

Legendre. Owner of that Mexican restaurant.

Vincent Smith. The weasel-eyed elevator operator in Pat's building.

Miss Copeland. In her 50s, she takes care of Helen's ill mother, **Mrs. Bishop.**

Tony. A helpful cab driver.

Officer Hornbuckle. A rookie policeman.

John Grape. A San Diego private eye who lends Pat a hand.

Books by Frances Crane

Featuring the Abbotts

The Turquoise Shop (1941)
The Golden Box (1942)
The Yellow Violet (1942)
The Pink Umbrella (1943)
The Applegreen Cat (1943)
The Amethyst Spectacles (1944)
The Indigo Necklace (1945)
The Shocking Pink Hat (1946)
The Cinnamon Murder (1946)
Murder on the Purple Water (1947)
Black Cypress (1948)
The Flying Red Horse (1950)
The Daffodil Blonde (1950)
Murder in Blue Street (1951)
The Polkadot Murder (1951)
Murder in Bright Red (1953)
13 White Tulips (1953)
The Coral Princess Murders (1954)
Death in Lilac Time (1955)
Horror on the Ruby X (1956)
The Ultraviolet Widow (1956)
The Buttercup Case (1958)
The Man in Gray (1958)
Death-Wish Green (1960)
The Amber Eyes (1962)
Body Beneath a Mandarin Tree (1965)

*Reprinted by the Rue Morgue Press

Non-Series Mysteries

The Reluctant Sleuth (1961)
Three Days in Hong Kong (1965)
A Very Quiet Murder (1966)
Worse Than a Crime (1968)

Non-Mystery

The Tennessee Poppy, or, Which Way Is Westminster Abbey? (1932)

The Shocking Pink Hat

A Pat and Jean Abbott mystery

Frances Crane

Rue Morgue Press
Lyons, Colorado

The Shocking Pink Hat
Copyright © 1946
ISBN: 978-1-60187-073-5

New material Copyright © 2012 by
The Rue Morgue Press
P.O. Box 4119
Boulder, CO 80306

www.ruemorguepress.com
800-699-6214

PRINTED IN THE UNITED STATES OF AMERICA

About Frances Crane

AFTER SHE WAS EXPELLED from Nazi Germany prior to the start of World War II, Frances Kirkwood Crane, recently divorced and with a daughter heading for college, needed to find a new way to make a living. The old market for her writing—primarily poking gentle fun at Brits from the point of view of an American living abroad—was suddenly out of fashion. Americans no longer wanted to laugh at the foibles of the English now that brave little Britain was engaged in a desperate struggle for its very survival against the forces of Hitler.

Up to that point, life had been relatively easy for Frances. Her husband, Ned Crane, was a well-paid advertising executive with the J. Walter Thompson agency, whose dubious claim to immortality was the Old Gold cigarette slogan, "Not a cough in a carload." Frances herself was a regular contributor to a new sophisticated humor magazine called *The New Yorker*. Many of her short sketches for that magazine were collected in book form in 1932 as *The Tennessee Poppy or Which Way Is Westminster Abbey?*

Back in the states, newly divorced and in need of money—living in the United States was more expensive than living in Europe—she had turned to the mystery field at the suggestion of one of her old editors who told her it was a "hot market." Not long after arriving in Taos, New Mexico, Crane, now around 50, heard about an incident involving a jewelry store in that artists' colony, which inspired her first Pat and Jean Abbott mystery, *The Turquoise Shop*, published by Lippincott in 1941. Although she changed the name of town to Santa Maria and even commented that it had not yet been spoiled in the fashion of Taos and Santa Fe, there is absolutely no question that it was based on Taos. In fact, Mona Brandon and her hacienda in *The Turquoise Shop* are loosely based on Mabel Dodge Luhan and her famous adobe home (now a bed and breakfast inn).

Jean Holly (she sounds terribly experienced and world weary, yet she's only 26) meets up with a handsome San Francisco private detective in that first novel. While Jean doesn't do any real sleuthing on her own, she functions as Pat's Watson and her careful observations, some only a woman of that era would make, bear close attention. *The Turquoise Shop* was followed by 25 more books featuring Pat and Jean Abbott, who marry toward the end of the third book, all with a color in the title. The series was so popular that it spun off a radio program, *Abbott Mysteries*, which ran on the Mutual Network in the summers of 1945, 1946 and 1947. Many of them take the Abbotts to locales across the United States and around the world, although they were to return to Santa Maria several times in the course of the series. *The Shocking Pink Hat* takes the Abbotts to San Francisco where is their home base. As usual, the locale is described in loving detail. Crane, who was expelled as a reporter from Germany in the late 1930s because of her open opposition to the Nazi's treatment of Jews, makes her usual quiet observations on race and ethnicity, this time in discussing Chinese-Americans. When Crane has a character describe someone as a "Chink" or use the "N" word in any of her books, you can be sure that he or she isn't going to be sympathetic. Crane's treatment of the Mexicans and Indians in New Mexico is handled in much the same way.

But Crane's intent was not to mount a soapbox. She wrote entertaining detective novels. Crane was quite familiar with the trends in contemporary detective fiction and was extremely well-read in the field. Along with fellow women mystery writers Lenore Glen Offord and Dorothy B. Hughes, she was one of the most influential mystery reviewers in the country, dwarfed in influence only by Anthony Boucher (for whom Bouchercon, the World Mystery Convention, is named). She relished her place in the literary world and numbered among her friends such literary lights as James Jones and Sinclair Lewis as well as her editor at Random House, the very urbane Bennett Cerf. Yet she realized she was not in that same league with these literary heavyweights, remarking once to Cerf that she was but a "minor light."

But all good things seemingly must come to an end. The Abbotts cracked their last case in 1965 with *Body Beneath the Mandarin Tree*. In the 1960s, Crane also wrote five stand-alone mysteries which were published in England but failed to find an American publisher. The last of these, *Worse Than a Crime*, appeared in 1968 when she was 78 years old, and though she would live another 13 years and enjoy relatively good health, her career as a mystery writer was over, and she settled into a well-earned retirement. Yet she had a better run than many women writers of her era, and, unlike most writers, male or female, she earned a good living at it. While many other female mystery writers who began in the 1930s and 1940s saw their careers end with the death of the rental libraries and the advent of the male-oriented paperback original in the early 1950s, Crane not only survived, publishing well into the 1960s, but endured, as any out-of-print book dealer who has ever offered one of her titles in a catalog and been overwhelmed with orders can testify. Her fans don't just enjoy her books, they revel in them, then and now.

She spent much of the last forty years of her life in her adopted New Mexico, mostly in Taos (though the "hippie invasion" in the 1960s drove her eventually to move to Santa Fe). She returned frequently to Lawrenceville to visit family. Three months before her 91st birthday, failing health forced her to enter a nursing home in Albuquerque, where she died on November 6, 1981. She made one final posthumous visit to Lawrenceville, a trip that many old-timers in that town still recall with amusement. The postmaster sent word to her nephew Bob, a local doctor, that a package had arrived for him from New Mexico. "Only," he explained, "you'll have to pick it up yourself. I'm not touching it."

The package was marked "human remains." Bob and other fellow family members scattered the ashes it contained on the family farm. Frances Kirkwood Crane not only came home, she did so in her usual unconventional style.

Note: For additional information on Crane and her connections to Taos read Tom & Enid Schantz' introduction to the Rue Morgue Press edition of *The Turquois Shop*.

The Shocking Pink Hat

ONE

The blonde woman at the table near ours was a smooth job in dark broadcloth and minks. She looked out of place in the Mexican-style jive-joint, which seemed to cater mostly to kids who yapped noisily about Scotch and soda but ordered less expensive concoctions mixed with vodka or inferior rum. The blonde had gilt hair, a really lovely oval face, a sweet smile and fine teeth. There was something peculiar about the expression of her blue eyes.

The man with her was distinguished-looking and he seemed upset. He kept pleading with the woman in a voice which never reached us on account of the din the imitation Mexican orchestra never stopped making. She apparently wore him down with silence. She continued to answer strictly nothing at all.

"That woman must be a so-and-so," I said to Patrick—my husband, Patrick Abbott, now back in San Francisco and for some mysterious reason on the inactive list after two years in the Intelligence Division of the U.S. Marine Corps. And just after having been made a Captain, too.

"Very stylish chick," he said.

"Chick?"

"Chick," said he, with that authority it is useless to buck. Even when you know he's mistaken.

Actually it was impossible to feel sure whether the woman was twenty or thirty. Even her eyes with their still, watchful, old look had the smooth flawless lids of a girl's.

The man was fortyish, tall, expensively tailored, with a longish face, gray eyes, a high white forehead and a nice amount of gray in his dark hair. He didn't look the kind to ask favors. But he never stopped his pleading unless the waiter was near, and that didn't happen very often because that waiter didn't seem to care if his customers were attended to or not. The waiter looked like a character. He was stooped, swarthy and gloomy-eyed. He moved like a sleepwalker. He would take your order and without a word stroll off through the dithering, jive-happy crowd in a dreamy fashion which made it seem quite a miracle that he got back successfully.

"I feel sorry for that gray-haired man," I said to Patrick.

His long blue-green eyes rested on me fondly.

"You're very sweet, darling."

"Seriously, she's got him in a spot, Pat."

Patrick said, "The first good case I get I'm going to buy you some emerald earrings. The real thing, to match that bracelet you keep in the bank."

I touched my synthetic numbers, which I happened to like very well.

"The first time you get a good case we'll be able to afford insurance on the bracelet and I'll take it out of the bank and wear it. No fooling, I'm worried about that man."

"You're beautiful, Jeanie. You're the only woman in the world with genuine amber eyes and jet-black hair. You're sweet."

"Pay attention to the poor gray-haired man, Pat!"

"I have," Patrick said. "He looks as if he can take it."

"Do you know him?"

"Never saw him before in my life. Want to dance? Shake a hip? Cut a rug? Swing it?"

"Darling?" I waved a hand at the squirming, perspiring mob on the handkerchief-sized dance-space. "Is it an affair, do you think?"

Patrick gave in. "My guess is they're married. I notice she wears a plain wedding ring and a not-too-large diamond. That would suggest that they got married when he hadn't the dough he's got now, which buys things like those minks. I'll buy you some minks after you have some more emeralds, Jeanie."

"I don't want any minks, dear. Go on about the man."

"Okay. She's all dressed up in her minks and obviously she expected to be taken to the Peacock Room instead of to a dive like this so she's giving him hell. She'll win. She's got a sweet mouth. He'll kiss her in the taxi and tomorrow he'll buy her a diamond necklace to go with those furs. I myself would buy emeralds."

I made a face at Patrick and slid another look at the pair.

The man was licked. There was something abject in his face. That expression didn't belong with his look of superiority. He took out a gold cigarette case. His hands, which had long slender fingers, trembled as he selected a smoke. He offered the case to the woman. She carelessly took a cigarette with a white hand whose over-long magenta-painted nails gave the impression of a hand of the dead. I shuddered. I do not usually have such morbid ideas. I glanced at Patrick. He was examining the pair, in his practiced fashion which makes him seem not to be observing anything at all. His eyes had assumed a vague faraway look.

The up-and-down sun-lines in his flat tanned cheeks were all at once obvious.

When the couple got ready to go, quite suddenly, I felt relieved.

The man tossed a bill on the table. The gloomy-eyed waiter drifted over and picked it up. The eyes of the two men met. There seemed to be an exchange, possibly of sympathy. Maybe the waiter's wife was also a shrew. No words were spoken, it was only an impression.

The woman used an unusual sense-stirring perfume. I caught it as they passed by our table. She walked with the gliding walk of a manikin, even in a crowded place like this. The man's shoulders drooped as he followed.

"Those minks are stunning," I said.

"I'll buy you some, baby."

"Darling! You've no idea! All our possessions put together—my emerald engagement ring and that emerald bracelet and your three little Renoir paintings you cherish more than you do me . . ."

"You've got those Renoir skin tones, Jeanie."

"Don't interrupt. That, plus my adobe house in New Mexico, plus all our war bonds and our other odds and ends, everything, all put together wouldn't buy that mink coat. Definitely, there's something odd about that pair."

"I agree," Patrick said, seriously.

"What is it, Pat?"

"I don't know. This whole set-up is queer, Jeanie. It's damn queer that when we ordered Scotch in this joint they brought us Scotch, of all things. I must look like a detective."

"How did we happen to come in here, anyway?"

"We were just walking by. You saw the donkeys and cactuses and sleeping Mexicans painted on the windows and it reminded you of New Mexico, so you wanted to come in."

"Well, it's a vicious, phony dump, Pat. Let's leave."

But we didn't leave for half an hour. Some kids who moved over to the table vacated by that striking couple started taking barbiturate tablets—goof-balls—along with a grape-juice vodka concoction they call a "purple passion." Patrick got interested in watching how they were getting the tablets, which can only be had by prescription in California. He didn't spot anything in particular, but it kept us a while longer in the dive. It was one o'clock exactly when we walked out of the place, and thirty minutes, I should say, after that couple had left.

The fresh salt-smelling air outside was wonderful. We turned right at Powell Street, keeping an eye out for a cab. It wasn't far to the furnished apartment we had found in a tall building on the brink of Russian Hill, but it was practically straight up from where we now were and I didn't want to climb all those stairs. It was situated near that spot where Green Street suddenly goes perpendicular, and where the street changes into a long flight of steps. On a clear night this nightlife section looked like a garden of rubies from our windows.

I glanced up, and wished I hadn't. Tonight the neons wouldn't even be visible. There was a thick fog sitting like a cap on the top of the hill.

Yet, down here, just below, the October air was crisp and perfectly clear. A small breeze blew off the bay.

We didn't find a cab. We walked along Powell to Washington Square and there caught the E-car up the hill. We got off at Union and Jones Streets. The only other passenger on the car was a patrolman who kept reading a small black-covered notebook. He also got off at Jones Street. After the car moved on we crossed Union to climb up Jones toward Green Street. The patrolman started patrolling down Jones Street toward the bay.

"A green one," Patrick said.

"A green what?"

"That patrolman. On the streetcar he was studying the Rules and Regulations."

"A detective is always detecting, dear."

"Yep. If he only knew in advance just what to detect his would be a happy lot."

"He would be very unhappy, just as anyone would be," I said. "It would be terrible to know everything in advance."

"It would indeed, Jeanie. You're right, dear. You're always right, darling."

"Idiot," said I.

He ducked his head and kissed my cheek.

That block between Union and Green on Jones Street is a honey. In any place save San Francisco it would be another job for stairs. But here it was a proper street, and motorcars traveled it up and down, just as though it were a normal thing to do.

Looking up what we could see of it, the block was tremendously steep. We could only see about half of it clearly, for the fog got very thick just above Macondray Place, which cuts through in the middle of this block. I hate the fog, and to delay our getting into it, for just a little, I suggested a last look at the view. We turned our backs to the hill and had a longish look. It was worth it. The streetlights made brilliant spangling patterns right down to the scalloped edge of blackness which was the bay. Beyond those waters the lights of Berkeley and Richmond shimmered up the hills. Alcatraz, near by, adequately lighted, was like a vast black forever-anchored ship. An old yellow moon stood above one span of the Bay Bridge. A real ship, identifiable only by its moving port and starboard lanterns, was sliding along between Yerba Buena Island and the mainland.

The new patrolman was walking very slowly a short way down the next block.

We turned—I reluctantly—and faced the fog.

Instantly Patrick stopped me.

A car was coming this way somewhere in that fog. It was impossible to know exactly where it was because sounds, as well as sights, are distorted by fog. There was something peculiar in its movement, a sort of hesitancy, a suggestion of groping. The motor was either amazingly quiet or dead. The noises the car made were the soft creakings from a well-kept chassis, and the rustling and whispery sounds of rubber tires against damp pavements.

We knew where it was exactly, however, when it reached the leveled intersection at Green and Jones Streets. All at once it came to a very brief stop, as if the driver had realized that a deadly fog-shrouded mist-slick descent was just ahead.

Then it plunged on down.

A big black convertible came out of the fog. It had no lights. The motor wasn't running. It was entirely out of control. It shot past us so quickly that I could see no one in it at all. We turned and watched it shoot on past Union Street, angle to the right and then crash into a hydrant near the end of the next block.

The patrolman was standing under a streetlamp. He stared at the wreck without making a move.

I said, "How horrible!"

Patrick emitted a string of the elegant oaths favored by the Marine Corps. He always got in a rage when people parked carelessly on these steep hills.

He said somewhat grudgingly that we'd have to go down and leave our names as witnesses of the accident. He said that considering the danger a runaway car is to others he hoped whoever was responsible would be caught and punished.

We started down.

We stopped again. Someone was walking this way, in the fog, someone who walked on cautious, anxious feet.

A dark form appeared not far above us. Then, as if spying us, it turned swiftly and ran with panicky scrambling steps back up the way it had come.

Patrick grabbed me by one hand and gave chase. After about ten feet he let my hand go and ran on without me.

TWO

Late the following afternoon Patrick and I sat by the window in the cocktail room on top of the Mark Hopkins Hotel drinking Manhattans and watching the drama set off by a clear sunset.

The waters of the bay and the ocean turned blue, then purple, then a doomful prune color. The brown hills and mountains were pink, lilac, finally dark gray.

The scene filled me with awe and humility.

"This town is simply terrific," I said.

Patrick's voice had the special tone it takes when he speaks of San Francisco. "It's swell."

"I should think you could rave harder than that, dear."

"That was raving," he said.

He was looking fine. His lean face with its flat sun-lined cheeks was a healthy tan color. His long eyes were very blue. His teeth were white and even, and his dark hair, which grows in a peak, looked positively crisp from good health.

He was in civs—a gray worsted suit, a blue-figured Sulka tie, which was one of a pre-war collection, and a blue shirt.

Patrick had been put on the inactive list presumably because of wounds he had received more than a year ago in the South Pacific. Privately I suspected he was secretly assigned to sleuth for the government in this vulnerable bay region. I didn't know, and I wouldn't be told the facts, of course, till military secrecy was no longer essential. He had arranged for desk space in the office of a friend and ostensibly he was free to do private business. But, though we certainly could use the extra money, he didn't seem in any great rush to pick up that extra dough. I didn't ask too many questions. It was too marvelous to have him here, and to be in the city we called home.

Garlands and blankets of lights began to shine around the deepening blackness which was the harbor. The night had come.

Inside the cocktail room the specially dimmed lighting made a kind of dusk, a twilight. Except at the point where a wedge of brightness from the entrance shone far enough in to light up a portion of the central bar, the room was so dim that it was hardly possible to distinguish faces at the next table. I was startled when a figure stood beside us and a deep, pleasant voice said,

"Hello, Pat. Heard you were back."

Patrick jumped up and put out a hand.

"Sam Bradish!"

"I'm mighty glad to see you, Pat."

"Same here."

They shook and shook. I sat trying to place Sam Bradish. I had certainly heard Patrick mention him. I couldn't think when, or how. In the dimness I could only make out that he was a big man with an agreeable voice and a well-cut brownish suit. Later, I made out his gray eyes, which always sparkled, his good-looking but determined mouth and ruddy cheeks. He was around forty.

"Jean, you've heard me speak of Sam Bradish. My wife, Inspector Bradish."

Oh, of course! Sam Bradish of the Bureau of Inspectors of the San Francisco Police Department! *The* Sam Bradish.

"How do you do, Inspector Bradish?"

"How do you do, Mrs. Abbott?"

"Won't you sit down?"

"Thank you."

Sam Bradish sat down. Patrick beckoned the waiter, who apparently could see in the dark. The Inspector ordered straight bourbon with a glass of water on the side. He offered cigarettes from the package, which were at this time already getting scarce. Half the time we could get none by the pack, and Patrick was regularly rolling his own, and some of mine too.

"Pat and I are old friends, Mrs. Abbott."

"I've heard him speak of you, Inspector Bradish."

Now I could see the gray eyes dancing. "Pleasantly, I hope?"

"Inspector Bradish!" Patrick said.

Bradish grinned. "Well, it's all in the game, Pat. Got an office yet?"

"None of my own. A friend has taken me in temporarily."

"Where's Lulu?"

Lulu Murphy was Patrick's former secretary.

"Still in Richmond. Still helping Kaiser make ships. Coming back to us when that job's over, I hope."

"You're out for good, I suppose?"

"Not if they need me, Sam."

"You don't look exactly unhealthy, Pat."

I said quickly, even though I agreed with the Inspector, "Pat was wounded pretty badly almost a year ago. He was a good while in the hospitals and then a while on convalescent leave and then assigned for three months light duty in New Orleans." It hadn't been light at all. And Pat was certainly in fine shape. But I was his wife and that was his story and by gosh I was going to stick to it, in public, at any rate. "He's all in one piece and everything, but I still worry about him no end, Inspector Bradish," I said.

The gray eyes sparkled hard.

"I'm glad you're keeping an eye on him, Mrs. Abbott. Don't let him settle down on top of one of our hills again. The wind, the fog, the rain."

Patrick pushed up one eyebrow.

"Which means, dear, that our friend Bradish has already found out we're settled on a hill. He's the kind of snake that checks up thoroughly in advance. Okay, Sam. What's cooking? Come clean."

Bradish grinned.

"Word had got around that you were back, Pat. I wanted to get in touch with you so I contacted Marine Headquarters, got the address of your temporary office, found out from some clerk that you were meeting your wife for a drink here at the Mark. That meant the Top of the Mark for kids your age at this time of day."

"Right on your toes, Inspector."

"No cracks, Pat," Bradish said.

Patrick fingered his cocktail glass.

"If you kept an eye on your accident reports you might have found my name and home address on Patrolman Hornbuckle's report for last night, Sam. But of course Homicide doesn't bother much with traffic accidents unless . . ."

The Inspector's voice took a somber tone.

"You said it, Pat. Unless it's murder."

Patrick said softly, "So it was murder."

"I say it was murder! Apparently the man had first been choked to unconsciousness and then a load of cyanide had been shot into the jugular vein. After that his car had been turned loose on that hill. Smart work. Only, why didn't you tell the nice new patrolman who the dead man was, Pat?"

"Dead man?" I said. "What dead man?"

"There was a man in that runaway car we saw last night," Patrick said, almost tenderly, as though I were the flowerlike kind. That was for Bradish.

"I didn't see anybody at all," I said.

"Neither did I. That is, until I got back down to the wreck."

My goodness! Patrick hadn't told me there was a body in that wreck. The man must have already been down between the seat and the instrument board when the car went past us on the hill. If he had been at the wheel we most certainly would have noticed him, no matter how fast the thing went.

Bradish cleared his throat.

"Patrolman Hornbuckle tells us that you didn't come down to the scene of the wreck for at least twenty minutes, Pat."

"Twenty minutes would be about right."

"Why wait twenty minutes?"

Patrick's eyes smiled.

"I took my wife home first, Inspector Bradish, sir."

Home, my eye! What a whopper! Patrick had cut loose from me after about five steps in that fog. I had had to find my way all by myself.

But I said, sweetly, "There was a terrible fog on our hill last night, Inspector Bradish. It sort of began all at once and it was thick as cotton. Pat was afraid I couldn't find my own way." You are being pretty wonderful, Jeanie, I complimented myself. You had a tough time getting home. You sat and fretted for an hour wondering why Pat didn't come in, wondering if he had caught the person he went after, wondering if some disaster had resulted.

And after all that Pat had double-crossed me! The heel! He hadn't said a word about there being a body in that car! Why not?

Patrick said, "I suppose the patrolman told you that we came up on the same streetcar, Sam? We were halfway up the block between Green and Union when the car rolled down the hill and crashed. Hornbuckle was near where it crashed. He was therefore right on the job and since neither of us saw anybody in the car there didn't seem any real reason for dragging my wife back down to the scene of the accident."

"I wasn't feeling too super," I said. Being the little woman. For the public.

Patrick gave me a fragment of a look, which warned not to overdo it, and then said, "I wouldn't've bothered to go down at all except to leave our names, Sam."

Even in the dim light I could see the Inspector's eyes sparkling like cold diamonds.

He said, "I sort of got it into my head that you dashed up for a cozy little chat with Mrs. Nancy Leland first. After which you went back down to the wreck."

Nancy Leland? She had been Nancy Moore when I'd first met her two years ago. Patrick had known her for ages.

Her brown shingle house was on Jones Street, about halfway up the block *above* Green. Jones wasn't so steep in that block, but steep enough that a car cut loose from the curb might start rolling downhill.

Bradish said, "The car probably started rolling in front of Nancy Leland's house. You happened to be on the hill. You recognized the car and went up to see what was what before getting down to the wreck."

"Did Nancy say so?" Patrick asked.

Bradish said, "She's not saying anything. She's sitting tight."

I was thinking, Well, Patrick did head toward Nancy's house when he ran off in the fog. Twenty minutes had passed. Bradish had a point there. I didn't get it. I felt furious with Pat, but I continued, I hope, to look wide-eyed and wifely.

Patrick's long blue eyes held Bradish's dancing gray gaze.

"You'll have to explain yourself, Sam."

"Mrs. Leland's a friend of yours, isn't she?"

"Of course she is. An old friend."

"That's what she said. I spent an hour or so with Mrs. Leland this afternoon. I went up there as soon as we knew who the dead man was, and was certain he had been murdered. She swears she didn't see him at all. Well, if he didn't go there to see her why would he be up there last night? At that hour? And in that fog? Incidentally, why didn't you tell Hornbuckle who the victim was, Pat? You could have saved us plenty of time."

"If I knew who the victim was I might better be able to answer you, Sam."

Bradish's voice ceased to be agreeable. His capable, well-kept hand gripped his glass hard.

"Aw, come off it, Pat. You know darn well that the dead man was Ernest K. Leland."

My breath felt tight in my chest. I stared at Patrick. He was looking at Bradish without the slightest change of expression on his good-looking face.

Lest I betray something I shouldn't, I quickly looked at the view. It was now all lights. Red lights, green lights, blue-white lights by the billion, and they all reminded me of Bradish's sparkling eyes.

I turned my attention to the interior of the cocktail lounge. It was shadowy, unreal, dimmed further than was planned by a fog of cigarette smoke. Then I noticed something special. Someone was standing in the narrow path of light from the entrance near the elevators. It was Gwen Telfer! Gwendolyn Telfer stood where the light fell clearly upon her and pointed at Inspector Bradish's back and shook her head at me and tapped her lips with a forefinger. Gwen signaled me to caution Patrick.

Gwendolyn Telfer was Nancy Leland's best friend.

Gwen Telfer also netted an easy thirty thousand a year handling the advertising of some of the businesses controlled by Ernest K. Leland. The *late* Ernest K. Leland.

"I'll be damned," Patrick said to Inspector Bradish. "So that was Ernest Leland."

"Was is right," Bradish said. "The corpse's face was not disfigured, Pat. Why did you hold out on Hornbuckle? Or why didn't you call me at once, if you didn't want to pass the information along to a patrolman? Or did you want to give Nancy Leland the time and opportunity to dream herself up a nice alibi? And therefore make yourself an accessory after the fact?"

"Has she an alibi?" Patrick asked.

"I don't know what she has or hasn't got," Bradish snapped. "She won't talk."

Oh, dear, I thought, wishing suddenly that we were in the ranching business, or running a curiosity shop as I used to do. Oh, dear.

Bradish said sarcastically, "Of course you didn't recognize the car, either. Not another like it in the city, but it meant nothing to you."

"Never saw it before," Patrick said.

Bradish's voice dripped irony.

"Serving with the army must have spoiled your fine touch, Pat."

"Navy, Sam. The marines are navy."

"Okay," Bradish said. He sounded annoyed. "I'll be sorry if I have to get tough, Pat, with your wife present . . ."

"I didn't know Ernest Leland, Sam. I'd never seen his car. That's my story and you can take it or leave it, just as you wish."

Bradish's mouth became hard and unpleasant. His shoulders hunched up like a halfback's. "Now, see here, Abbott. No tricks. I like you, see. You've always played a clean game, or almost always, but if you've gone and got yourself tangled up in this thing . . . Oh, I'll admit that Mrs. Leland is a mighty pretty young woman, charming, too, and of course maybe there are extenuating circumstances—but she'll come into a lot of money—you always had a hearty interest in the dough . . ."

Gwen Telfer cleared her throat so effectively that the sound carried to me through all the din. I glanced at her. She was still behaving in the same way, pointing at Bradish, making faces, shaking her head.

Patrick said, "I told you I had never before seen Leland, Sam. That's true. But if I had known who he was when I saw him in that wreck last night I most certainly would have gone up to see Nancy. And I would have also called you. Or your department, which is—I was about to say all the same thing, but of course that's absurd. There is only one Sam Bradish."

I didn't know if Pat was being sarcastic or not. But Bradish let it pass. "So you don't deny knowing Nancy Leland?"

"Certainly not."

"How long have you known her?"

"I've known her ten years at least, ever since she was a young kid. I knew her father when he was alive, and I know her brother Rufus Moore. Nancy married Ernest Leland after we left San Francisco and was separated from him before we came back, which is how it happens we hadn't met Leland."

"Seen Nancy since you got back? I don't mean last night."

"Twice. And she spoke pleasantly about her husband. She did say the marriage was ended. There was no reason for her to explain why. She said she wanted us to meet Leland. I believe he's been away."

"They're not divorced," Bradish said, almost petulantly.

"I know nothing about that."

Gwen Telfer again cleared her throat. When I looked that time she shook her taffy-colored head so hard the cobalt-blue feathered hat she wore jiggled like a cork. Then she buttonholed one of the azure-jacketed waiters, pointed at us, gave him a tip, looked back at me, and pointed at the waiter. He nodded several times. Gwen left the room. The waiter promptly dropped the money in his pocket and walked over to another table.

Bradish was still talking.

"It was you yourself who planted the idea in Hornbuckle's mind that Leland had been murdered, Pat. If you hadn't done that, the business might have got by as a traffic accident. That was obviously what was intended by the murderer. The marks on the throat were very slight. The man was apparently strangled only to the point of unconsciousness. The needle in the hypo used was very fine; it made a mere prick on the throat. Since it pierced the jugular vein its victim probably died instantly. Cyanide leaves its victims so natural-looking that, if the patrolman hadn't been tipped off, there would not have been a post mortem. There was no cyanide odor until they opened up the body. We're too damn busy to do autopsies unless murder is pretty obvious. Leland's body would have been claimed, and no doubt cremated and no one would ever have known what killed him."

"Well, you might at least give me credit for putting Hornbuckle on the right track, Sam. Look, would I run up to warn Nancy Leland, and then afterwards go back down the hill and tell the patrolman it looked like murder?"

"Maybe you got cold feet."

"Nope. I didn't go to see Nancy, and I didn't get cold feet. But when

I got back down to the wreck Hornbuckle was in a state. It was his first night on the job and in fact the very first block of his first beat. He had never before witnessed a serious accident of any kind. Like ourselves, he hadn't seen the man when the car was rushing down the hill. He discovered him when he went to look at the wreck. Leland wasn't banged up much, had not bled at all, was still warm, and Hornbuckle didn't realize that he was dead. He spent a few minutes getting him out of the wreck. That's a lonely block at that hour. Nobody came by while he was getting Leland out on the ground. He left him then and went to a drugstore a block away and called Headquarters for an ambulance. All this happened before I arrived. I'm quoting Patrolman Hornbuckle. When I got there they were just putting the body in the police ambulance. A few people had gathered around the car. Hornbuckle still didn't realize that Leland was dead. He had taken no papers or anything from him for identification. The ambulance pulled away at once. We looked through the glove box after the body was taken away, but there was nothing there that helped any, so he wrote down the license number to be checked from the police station. The car was a big special body Lincoln, or had been before it was a mass of junk, and I suggested Hornbuckle might perhaps find out who owned it by telephoning garages around town."

Bradish was getting restless.

"Yeah, but why did you suggest it might be murder?"

"Routine. You know I think there ought to be autopsies in all cases of death by violence, Sam. I like to feel sure. I thought maybe the man had died of a heart attack up on the hill. I would want to know, definitely. Frankly, I had no real honest-to-goodness reason to suspect murder."

Except that someone ran away into the fog, I thought.

But I didn't say so. I kept very still. I wondered if the waiter Gwen had given the tip would come over and deliver her message. He had vanished. Would he come back? Would I recognize him if he did come back? Well, it probably wasn't anything to bother about. Gwen was a great one for running other people's affairs. She was probably just sticking her chic nose into this one for excitement.

Patrick said, "Why the hell were you so long getting busy on this case, Sam?"

On the defensive, Bradish was less formidable.

"Well, we're rushed. You know that. Got about half as many men on the force as we need, the way the city's packed and jammed these days. Then Hornbuckle bungled the job, even after your tip-off. He put you down as P. Abbot, without any address. He didn't turn in the report for hours. The first hint we got about who the corpse in the morgue might be was when they identified the car as belonging to Ernest K. Leland. I got onto the job then and went around to the morgue and examined the body. Leland's papers were in his pocket. They included his driver's license, various insurance cards and such, and the remains of an airplane ticket from Mexico City. The portion of the ticket from Los Angeles to San Francisco hadn't been used. We checked and found he had missed connections in L.A. and had picked up a private plane. Some dame came up with him from L.A., but the pilot who flew them didn't know who she was, thought maybe it was his wife. It wasn't; description doesn't fit. Besides, Nancy Leland was at her job yesterday afternoon and she says she was not at home all last evening. Among Leland's papers was one of those diplomatic visas the Mexican government sometimes hands out to Americans who do a lot of business down there, a kind of courtesy, I guess, to pass them quickly through the customs. He must have made the trip pretty often. Mrs. Leland admitted it. After checking his papers I stayed around while the medical examiner went over the body. Then I went to see his wife. She's got a job out at Fort Mason and didn't come in for a while. A Chinese housekeeper let me in, and kept her eye on me while I waited, too."

"Did you tell Nancy Leland her husband had been murdered?"

"Did I need to tell her, Pat?"

"I really don't know, Sam."

Bradish shrugged. "I gave it to her straight. She looked kind of stunned. That Chinese woman hovered in the hall, like a mother."

"She is like one, Sam. She's been there since Nancy was a baby. What did Nancy say?"

"What she said," Bradish said crossly, "was nothing plus. She shut up like a clam, shock or no shock. I asked her if she wouldn't come into a nice hunk of cash from Leland's death and she said she really didn't know or care."

"Nancy has quite a temper."

"Well, temper or not, she left him and there hasn't been a divorce and apparently she stands to come into plenty. She's hard up. She admitted that. She says that house of hers is mortgaged. Why did she and Leland separate?"

"She never told me, Sam."

"She told me," Bradish said. He sniffed it. "She told me they were uncongenial."

"That would be enough, wouldn't it?"

This time the inspector snorted.

"She said they stayed married only six months. Why didn't she get a divorce? She said he hasn't been supporting her since she left him."

"I wouldn't know anything about that, Sam."

"She asked me," Bradish said, with a puzzled glance, "if he had suffered. I said she probably knew as much about that as anybody, since it seems she's a laboratory worker of some kind and would probably know something about cyanide. It wouldn't be hard for her to pick up the poison out there where she works. It doesn't take much. Anybody in Leland's confidence could have done the deed itself. It only takes a few seconds—a little pressure on the carotid artery—unconsciousness—a fine hypo. But she ran out of luck when the body wasn't mangled in the crash." Bradish showed signs of planning to move on. "There isn't the slightest question in my mind that Nancy Leland did it, Pat."

"The trouble is, you'll have to prove it."

"I'll prove it!"

Patrick spoke, after a small silence.

"Are you charging her with the murder?"

"In due time."

"Well, don't rush it, Sam. You'll feel mighty silly if it turns out Nancy didn't do that dirty work."

Bradish asked invitingly, "What makes you think she didn't?"

"What makes you think she did?"

"I've told you. She had the means, the motive—his money and her freedom—and the opportunity. What more do you want?"

"Proof."

Bradish picked up his whisky glass and tapped it lightly on the table, and, giving Patrick a sparkling look, asked, "How come you did nothing about the hat?"

"Hat?" I said.

The Inspector politely ignored me. "Why did you leave that red-feathered hat of Mrs. Leland's there in the back of the car, Pat? You could have grabbed it easy as that." He snapped his fingers. "Hornbuckle would have been too bothered to take any notice."

I restrained an impulse to correct him about the color of the hat. I knew that hat. It wasn't red. It was rose-colored, a rich rose called shocking pink by some, a vivid-feathered hat. It was a mate for that blue-feathered number Gwendolyn Telfer was wearing this afternoon when she stood yonder signaling us to be careful about what we told Sam Bradish. Gwen had given the hat to Nancy Leland. I had seen it in its box, but I had not seen Nancy wearing it.

Bradish said, "We've got the hat. Well, the milliner who made that hat says it was delivered to Mrs. Leland ten days ago, which was after Leland went to Mexico. We find it in his car, see, which Mrs. Leland swears she has not used, has not even seen since he left. How come her new hat rolled down that hill last night along with Leland's dead body?"

Patrick made no reply. He sat without moving, it might have been without feeling or thinking. Maybe he was shocked almost to immobility, as I was. Damn, I thought, that hat!

Bradish got up. He was affable now. He had made his point. How big he looked. How powerful. How sure of himself.

"I'll be seeing you soon, Pat. I've got your phone number at the house. The clerk gave it to me when I called your office. Sorry to have to be so frank in front of you, Mrs. Abbott. I'm so busy I can't take time to handle anything with gloves nowadays."

Patrick had risen. We shook hands with the Inspector. He had a warm-feeling hand, very friendly.

"Murders keeping you so busy, Sam?"

Bradish shrugged. "Murders and the things that cause murders," he said. "Come down and look at the big honor roll in the chief's office and you'll realize why I haven't got time to think these days." He bowed to me. "Good-bye, Mrs. Abbott. So long, Pat."

THREE

So much had been said that I forgot for two or three minutes after Inspector Bradish was gone that I'd been waiting for him to beat it so I could put my husband on the mat. But I got around to it pretty pronto. "Why didn't you tell me there was a body?" I demanded then.

"It must have slipped my mind, Jean."

"It did *not*!"

"I didn't want to upset you, then."

"You didn't want me quizzing you, you mean. You win, darling. Was it awfully banged up?"

"Not at all. But it was certainly dead."

I said, "You knew it was Leland, of course."

"I certainly didn't."

"You said you'd never seen it before?"

"Not that precisely, did I?"

"Patrick, are you withholding information from that detective? Are you being an accessory after the fact?"

"Certainly not, my love. Like another drink?"

"Nope." I was simply crawling with suspicion. "You did go up to Nancy Leland's when you left me there in the fog, didn't you, dear? Please note I said left. Not cast me off, or abandoned. You weren't very gallant."

"I'm very sorry."

"You didn't know even if I got home safely. . . ."

"Oh, yes, I did. I stopped back and asked the elevator man if you had arrived all right. He said you had, though I don't know why I took his word for it. That elevator man looks like a rat."

"Never mind him now, dear. You really didn't suspect when we saw the car that it was murder?"

Patrick smiled upside-down. "I'm not divine, baby. But I did get a notion that the car had been deliberately wrecked, maybe to claim some insurance or something. There was something queer about the way it hesitated at the intersection, as though somebody just stepped out and then let it roll. Then there was the odd behavior of whoever it was faded off in the fog."

"Was that a man or woman?"

"I never got close enough to tell."

"You *really* didn't go to Nancy Leland's?"

Patrick inhaled, and took his time. My insistence annoyed him, so he paid me back by letting me dangle.

"Nope. I didn't go to Nancy's. I did go up Jones that far, though. Her front lights were on. They showed up like two blurs in the fog. I was tempted to go in and ask if she had noticed anything suspicious but just then I heard footsteps again—the same fussy jittery kind we'd heard on the hill, and this time across the street and slipping back down toward Green Street—so I tailed said steps down to and along Green Street to a point near the fire station where they again ceased. There's a big front yard next the fire station where the gate usually hangs open and which has a lot of shrubbery and my suspect could have hidden there, I suppose, or, for that matter, any of the gardens on that side of Green would have given him cover. . . . Anyway, about that time, it occurred to me that the smart thing was to get back down to the wreck and leave my name and mention my suspicions if there was an investigation of the affair. I was nuts to run after anyone in a blind fog."

"It would have been all right if he had gone to a house, and gone in."

"Thanks for the kind thought, Jeanie. I don't deserve it."

I waited a moment.

"Why do you suppose Nancy had her front lights on? At that hour?"

"Maybe she forgot them."

"You didn't tell Inspector Bradish about those lights."

"No."

"And you fibbed to him about taking me home."

"Uh-huh."

"Why?"

"I hated to have him know how I treat my wife."

I let that pass.

"You're sure you didn't go to see Nancy, Pat?"

"Pretty sure. Why should I? I had no idea the accident could be tied up with her in any way."

I allowed a small interval to pass.

"It was right polite of me, don't you think, not to tell the nice detective about your chasing after somebody in the fog?"

"It was lovely, Jean. I'd hate having Bradish know I was so dumb. I'll buy you another drink right now just because you're a pal, and have yaller eyes, wonderful hair . . ."

"Darling, I don't want another drink. This is terribly serious! That Bradish is smart, I'll bet. I'm afraid Nancy Leland is in for a lot of trouble. She's a swell gal. I hate to think of her in a spot like this. I think you ought to help her."

A waiter approached us and gave us Gwendolyn Telfer's message, which was that she was expecting us to dine with her at Jack's, and would like us to come along at once. "If you can't make it, please telephone the lady at Jack's," the man said. Patrick tipped him, beckoned our own waiter, found that Bradish had paid the bill, looked tickled at getting a drink off the police department, and tipped that waiter too.

We left the Top o' the Mark. Twenty stories down, crossing the hotel lobby, I said, "You didn't tell me that Gwen had asked us to dinner tonight."

"You didn't tell me, Jeanie."

It went against the grain.

"Isn't that just like her! Let's not go!"

"I'd hate missing a chance to eat at Jack's," Patrick said. "Besides, I want to talk to Gwen."

He held the door for me to go outside.

"I saw her come into the cocktail lounge, Pat. She stood in the lighted spot near the door and made signs for us not to tell things to Bradish. I wonder . . ."

"I saw Gwen," Patrick said.

We stepped out on the triangular spot where the taxi-cabs pull up at the front entrance of the Mark Hopkins Hotel. A long line waited for transportation. Up California Street a bell clanged and we saw, coming our way, a cable car, looking like a pincushion from its overload of passengers, but we sprinted for it and squeezed into a foothold on the outside steps. We dropped off at Montgomery, walked to Sacramento, and back half a block to Jack's. Gwendolyn Telfer and Philip Hannegan sat at a table for four halfway back in the little French restaurant. Gwen's jewel-like turquoise eyes spotted us instantly and she lifted an arm to greet us. Philip Hannegan stood up and held my chair. Phil was almost as tall as Patrick, broader in the shoulders, blond, with deep blue eyes under dark brows and fair smooth hair. After three years on the Western Front he had cracked up over the Ardennes, and had been put on the inactive list three or four months ago. He still walked with a slight limp. Though I didn't know him very well I had made up my mind he was rather stubborn. Gwen Telfer apparently thought she was in love with him.

Gwen was small, straightbacked, with a heart-shaped face, that taffy-reddish hair, and those jewel eyes, so exquisitely set and always in motion. Her sun-tan had a rosy hue and was maintained in foggy San Francisco by sun-lamp. She was wearing a tailored suit in the same rich blue as her small feathered sailor. A short fur cape was slipped down over the back of her chair.

"How about steaks, French fries, green peas and ordering whatever dessert you want later?" Gwen said efficiently, beckoning the waiter as she talked and we got ourselves settled. The cocktails got ordered efficiently. "Now, the wines. They've got real French claret and burgundy," Gwen announced. "Whichever you want. Salads, everybody? Fine." The waiter was hovering in attendance, ready to be off with the order as soon as Gwen had given it. She gave him a fine smile. "Please hurry, Jules." He bobbed his sleek head and was gone. "Look, Pat, wasn't that Inspector Bradish with you at the Mark? Was he talking about the murder? He thinks Nancy did it. Did he tell you so?"

Phil Hannegan said, "Maybe he doesn't really think that, Gwen. Maybe he was bluffing." He sounded anxious, though. He had been at Nancy Leland's both times we had been since coming back. They had made a nice pair. I had somehow got the idea that it meant something. But here was Gwen, acting as though she had him hog-tied.

"Well, Nancy's in a spot, whatever he thinks, Phil. And she will not listen to reason. Pat, I want you to take her case."

"Does she want me?" Patrick asked. He had taken out the cigarette makings and was rolling us cigarettes. The action irked Gwen, who urged hers on us, insisting she had plenty, and I accepted one, but Patrick stuck to his own.

"Nancy doesn't know what she wants," Gwen said. "That's her trouble. She does the wrong things. She married Ernest Leland because she had a father complex. It didn't click. That's okay, plenty of gals make that mistake. She hadn't divorced Ernest plainly and simply because she knew he didn't want her to. Or that's how I dope it out. I adore Nancy, but she is a dilly, Pat. She's old-fashioned. She's spent too much time with people too much older than herself. Her father. Her brother Rufus, who is sixteen or seventeen years older than Nancy, as you know. I guess she thought she wanted Ernest Leland, who was crowding forty when she was only twenty-two, and she went ahead and married him. Against my advice, too. Mind you, I adored Ernest, but I *do understand people* and I knew in advance those two wouldn't click. The marriage lasted six months, broke up, and there you are. But she's still—was, I should say—legally his wife. Well, just try to explain all that to policemen! You know how they are!"

Philip Hannegan said, somewhat acidly, "I'm told some of them are quite intelligent, Gwen."

Gwen cast him a fond glance.

"Darling! Of course. But Nancy and Ernest haven't lived together for some time. And they did not go ahead on that divorce, even though they didn't openly quarrel about it. Also—and this is the worst—he made a will lately leaving everything to Nancy except a small trust fund to be held for his son."

"Son?" I said.

"Ernest was married the first time when he was just a kid. They were divorced. That wife died three years ago. Phil thinks I'm overimaginative. I'll tell you all about it just as soon as you promise me you'll take the case."

"Do I have to promise before I get the dope, Gwen?"

"The information is confidential. I took it for granted that you would do anything to save Nancy."

Not even Nancy, if she did murder, I thought.

The waiter came back with the cocktails and then with small loaves of fresh French bread and the thin rationed pats of sweet butter, and then he filled the water glasses.

Philip Hannegan remained silent, but Gwen said conversationally, "I hear you've got a swell place to live."

"It's entirely too swell," I said. "They won't let us have our cat and dog there."

"I hate animals," Gwen said. "They waste your time. Well, cheerio!"

We picked up the cocktails.

Patrick said, when the waiter had gone, "Was Leland expecting to die, Gwen?"

"Gosh, no. Why?"

"You spoke about his will."

"Oh, that. He was always making wills. He made this one because he was going to let Nancy get the divorce and he wanted her to have his money anyway. You see, he was crazy about Nancy, whether she liked him or not. In his way, he was mad about her."

"In his way," said Philip Hannegan.

"My dear, he merely wasn't demonstrative."

"I see," Philip said.

"Well, anyway, he wanted Nancy to have his money and since he led a hazardous life . . ."

"How come?" Patrick asked.

"Oh, he was always flying places, and driving like mad. Always taking chances. He had his finger in I don't know how many pies. My God, he made money. Well, there you are. It goes to Nancy. So what will people think?"

"How do you know the contents of the will?" Patrick asked.

"I was a witness. Ernest let me read the will, asked me to do so, in fact. I'm tipping you off now in advance because when it's made public Nancy will be in a worse spot than ever."

"Nancy doesn't give a damn about his money," Philip said.

Gwen nodded.

"Phil, you're right. You're definitely right. But will the police believe that? Of course not. He was rich when they got married and he was too old for her and she was broke. They'll draw the obvious conclusions. Let's waive all that and get down to facts. Ernest got in town last night, late, and called Nancy up and was evidently on his way up there, or something, when he got murdered."

"How do you know he phoned her?" Patrick asked.

"She told me so," Gwen said. "When we got word at the office that he was dead—the police didn't tell us it was murder at first—I rang her up. Naturally. She said Ernest called her about half-past twelve last night and wanted to see her at once. She got up and dressed and turned on the front lights on account of the fog but he never showed up. Fortunately, she didn't tell this to Inspector Bradish. She said she forgot to. She said she was so shocked when he told her Ernest was dead that she hardly knew where she was. I made her promise she wouldn't tell him. She listened to me when I reminded her that it would be even worse for her brother Rufus than for her because naturally any unfavorable publicity is sure to cost Rufus his job."

"Why?" Patrick asked.

"Rufus manages the office Ernest maintained in Los Angeles for sort of pooling the Leland interests. There's nothing of that sort here, most of his investments are centered in the southern part of the state. We do his advertising and he lived here, at the Royal Palace Hotel, but the money is made down there. If Nancy is mixed up in this murder the other directors will get rid of Rufus. He's not so good at his job, you see. Anyway, when Nancy telephoned me this afternoon . . ."

"You telephoned her," Philip said.

"Right," Gwen said agreeably.

Patrick and I were again drinking Manhattans. Gwen's cocktail was a Martini. Philip Hannegan had a Bacardi. His well-shaped brown fingers kept gripping the stem of his glass so hard I expected it to snap.

Gwen said, "Of course I did, Phil. I called Nancy. I didn't mean to imply anything else."

"Did you know Leland was coming in last night?" Patrick asked Gwen.

"Well, yes. Only he didn't arrive when we expected him."

"He was supposed to come back on the plane I took from Los Angeles late yesterday afternoon," Philip said.

"Ernest missed his connection and chartered a private plane," said Gwen.

"How could he rate a private plane?"

"He's up to his eyes in defense plants," Gwen said. "If anybody on the Coast rated a private plane whenever he wanted he was it. But he seldom used one, just the same."

"He was accompanied here by a woman," Patrick said. "Bradish told us that."

There was a silence, a quick interchange of glances, two pairs of eyes suddenly full of real or exquisitely faked surprise.

"Who was she?" Gwen asked, trying to look more casual than she sounded.

"The police don't know who she was. Leland had wired ahead and had his car sent out to the airport . . ."

"He always did that," Gwen said. "Lately, with the military grabbing plane seats, Ernest wasn't sure just when he might get in so he would wire his garage to send out the car and leave it for him. He carried an extra set of keys and the car sat and waited till he arrived."

"He must have had a C-card," I said.

Philip said, "If there was anything to be had, Leland had it. You can be sure of that."

Gwen registered a weak protest.

"But, darling, as I just said, he was up to his ears in defense. He rated any privileges he got."

Patrick asked, "Why had he been in Mexico?"

There was a split second in which neither answered the question, as if each knew the answer but hesitated to speak it, and then Gwen said, "Look, that can wait. It was all on the up and up, however, strictly business. What I wanted to tell you is that we know who murdered Leland and if you'll jump right in and grab him quick it might be possible not to let Nancy get dragged into it at all." Gwen leaned forward and said, in a whisper, "His son killed him."

Philip looked bored. "Really, Gwen!"

"Oh, darling, please! You like Nancy, don't you, Phil?"

There was something so artless, so childish, in the question that I cast an inquiring look at Philip, and then looked down my nose, for I realized all at once that Phil *loved* Nancy. Surely Gwen could read the meaning of the anguish which suddenly filled his deep-blue eyes. What was all this? Was I wrong about Gwen? Wasn't she making a play for Hannegan, as I thought? Or was she being splendid about Nancy Leland, knowing all the time she was a rival, and that her own was a losing game? Or didn't she even know it? My goodness!

"I would not accuse that kid of murder just because I like Nancy," Philip said. "There are plenty of people who might have had cause to kill Leland."

"But, Phil, that boy looked so utterly fantastic. . . ."

"He looked exactly like any college kid these days. They all get themselves up like tramps. Chris Leland wore the customary baggy flannel pants, tweed jacket, loud shirt, and dirty raincoat."

"But his hair and all? He has red hair, Pat, and it stands straight up. Freckles. A funny little nose . . ."

"I liked his face," said Philip.

"He had that gun, Phil?"

"Gun?" Now I was leaning forward, all interest, for guns really hypnotize me, like snakes.

Philip said, "Leland was murdered with cyanide, Gwen."

"But Chris told us he was studying science," Gwen argued. "Maybe the gun he showed us was a blind? Maybe he had the cyanide in a pocket all the time?"

Her voice was pliant, it bent to make a question at the end of each sentence. My goodness! The play the wonder-girl was making for Philip Hannegan would have been ham in a gal of sixteen. She was his in every flicker of her trim eyelashes, every intonation of her smartly styled voice, every movement of her chic small shape.

I felt a little sorry for her all at once, and also disillusioned, because my awe of Gwen Telfer was melting away fast. In my mind, I summed up her story. She had come to San Francisco when eighteen from some town in the San Joaquin Valley, equipped with a high school education, the ability to take shorthand and type, beautiful eyes and a vast amount of determination. In six years she had worked herself up to being called the leading advertising woman in the city. She was now twenty-seven.

There was definitely an impasse. These two differed, in the matter of young Chris Leland, and I wondered if Gwendolyn would give in to please Philip. In that case, what would happen to Nancy?

Patrick spoke up suddenly, asking a question. "Did you like Leland, Phil?"

Gwen answered. "Everybody liked Ernest," she declared. "By the way, I might tell you at this point, in case there's any doubt in your mind, Pat, that the pay for tracking down the murderer won't be peanuts. You can name your own price. You must be pretty hard up after all your time in the service, Pat."

Patrick made a little nod and said for the second time, "Did you like Ernest Leland, Phil?"

Philip Hannegan's striking blue eyes met Patrick's. They stayed there, leveled and unchanging. Gwen sat forward in her chair, her breast thrust out and up as if she dared not go on with her normal breathing till she heard what Philip might say.

   He said nothing. He thrust a hand in one pocket, brought out his cigarettes, and busied himself entirely with lighting one.

FOUR

Evidently Gwendolyn Telfer would rather please Philip Hannegan than persist in bringing young Christopher Leland to justice. It became obvious almost abruptly. We did learn, however, that Chris was seventeen years old and that he had come to Gwen's office in an attempt to locate his father. His parents had been separated since he was three years old. He had started his freshman year at Yale this autumn but had flunked out. He had procured the gun he carried from a friend, and had come all the way to San Francisco to shoot his parent. He had located Leland's hotel somehow and had been referred to Miss Telfer for information on Leland's current whereabouts. He had gone then to her office. Gwen had been frightened and had asked Philip's aid in getting the boy out of the office without making a scene. Philip had then talked to young Chris in his own office, and had taken away the gun.

Gwen said, "Phil put it in a drawer and then was called out of the office a minute and evidently Chris got it again and took it away."

Philip said, "I was so convinced that he was harmless that I didn't even think of the gun again. I left him sitting by my desk. He was sitting where he'd been when I got back to my office. I didn't look in the drawer where I had put the gun. Later I left the office with the kid to help him find a room—you know what a chore that is these days."

"When was all this?" Patrick asked.

"Day before yesterday. Late in the afternoon."

Gwen said, "Phil flew down to L.A. yesterday morning without even coming to the office. He didn't know the gun was missing from his desk till he got back this morning."

Patrick said, "What kind of gun?"

"A Colt automatic .32-calibre."

They're horrid-looking guns. I shuddered.

"Loaded?" Patrick asked.

"I think so," Philip said. "It felt heavy enough to be fully loaded. I saw that the safety catch was on and put it in the drawer."

"Could anyone else have taken it?"

"Sure. The desk wasn't locked. Neither was my office door. I was away all day yesterday."

"Did you call young Chris when you got back?"

Philip nodded. "Right away. He left the hotel just before noon yesterday. He had no luggage and had to pay for his room in advance. I'm afraid he's got no money and is maybe sleeping out somewhere. I think I was criminally negligent not to find out if he had any cash."

"Poor boy," Gwen said, and it didn't quite come off. And as though she knew that, she added, "Even though he did seem deranged. Loopy, you know."

And then, just as if she now wanted it that way, her interest in the case had petered out. Maybe it was the delicious food and the wines, making us feel happy, giving us the illusion that all was well in the world. Maybe it was because she hadn't expected Philip Hannegan to buck her plans. And she did not want to buck Philip. And, really, why should it matter to Gwen if Nancy was accused or not? Why did she want to avert any scandal? Yet, that might easily be answered. Any reflection on anything connected with Leland might affect the business and cause Gwen some loss. Perhaps a great loss.

Whatever it was, as the meal progressed it was Gwen Telfer who took the least interest in what she had started, or rather tried to start.

As we came out of Jack's a cab rolled up. Patrick hailed it when it was free and proposed that we take the slightly longer route home via California Street, so as to drop Gwen at the apartment hotel where she lived on top of Nob Hill, and Hannegan at his house not far from ours on Russian Hill.

Philip said fine. A sudden furrow between Gwen's well-groomed brows deepened, and then vanished as another cab, with its flag up, rolled in back of ours.

"We've got to stop by the office," she said. "Come along, Phil. Goodbye, kids. So grand you could come, and all."

Their cab pulled around ours and got away first.

It moved fast. When we turned the corner and started toward California Street they were almost a block ahead and pulling up for a red light. The cab was in the right lane, ready for turning up Nob Hill.

Then, as we drew near, Gwen leaned forward and said something to their driver and when the green light came on he drove straight ahead as he would have done in the first place if she had asked him to take them to the office.

We turned up Nob Hill on our way home.

The air was clear and sparkling. The great hotels on top of the hill were tiers of scattered lighted oblongs reaching high into the sky.

Two cable cars moved on the hill, one toddling up, one coming down. Behind each the cable in the pavement crackled and sparkled. Up-going auto traffic moved violently fast, San Francisco style, making its run for the steep hill.

"I guess Gwen gave us the brush-off," I said.

Patrick said, "She wanted to be alone in a taxi with Phil." He put his arm around me and kissed me. "No place like a taxi," he said.

Presently, I said, "I expect she thought we would go home the other shorter way and not catch her pulling a trick. Why didn't we, incidentally?"

"Maybe we wanted to see if Gwendolyn really went to her office."

"Don't you trust her, Pat?"

"Nope. Do you?"

"I don't like her at all. And I admire her awfully."

"Um-m."

"Why didn't we follow and see where they went?"

"It's not very important, is it? I'm sure she only wanted to be with Phil. She felt they had disagreed, and she wanted him to cool off before he went home. Maybe they'll just ride around. Maybe they'll really go back to the office."

"She's certainly out to snare him."

"God help him," Patrick said.

I said, "Phil didn't like Ernest Leland, Pat."

"I think you're right."

"And Gwen knows it. I'll bet she wanted to caution him about it."

We were stopped by a light at Stockton Street. We moved on. I asked Pat why he said God help him about Phil. Because if Gwen made up her mind to get Phil she'd probably get him, he said. Didn't he think Gwen attractive? I asked, and he said that in her way she was attractive as hell. I asked what was wrong with her then and he said she had no sex appeal and that also she always made you feel she was smarter than you were. I said that wasn't smart and Patrick grinned and kissed me. The driver watched us in his little mirror. We were now passing the Fairmount Hotel. Patrick leaned forward and asked the man to pull into the filling station at the top of Nob Hill and park at a place where the cab would be screened by the shrubbery but still have a view down the street. A lush grin crooked up the man's cheek and stayed there, and he must have been disappointed, if counting on romance, when Patrick glued his face to the rear window the minute we got located and stared at Gwen's apartment hotel close by.

Not for long. In just about the time it takes to circle a city block which is fairly deserted at night, Gwen's cab pulled up at her entrance. The doorman scampered under the striped awning to open the cab door. He beat it back to the front door and opened it for Gwen while Philip Hannegan was paying the fare. The man held the big shining plate-glass door open until Philip followed Gwen inside.

I said to Patrick, "Now what do you think?"

"I'm thinking it's amazing that there are still such doormen in the world," Patrick said, and he pushed open the window to ask the cabman to drive on.

At the Cathedral we turned into Jones Street and climbed again. The lights kept sparkling and the leaves of the trees around the reservoir on Hyde Hill danced in a light breeze. Nevertheless, the darkness thickened because the street lamps were spaced farther apart.

We dropped down to Pacific Street and climbed back up again on Russian Hill. We passed by Nancy Leland's dark shingle house. Its windows glowed peacefully behind closed venetian blinds.

Across the street stood a man in a white raincoat.

We both glanced back as our cab made the turn at Green Street. The man still stood, exactly where we had seen him, and perfectly visible because there was a street lamp near by.

"Do you suppose he's watching Nancy?" I asked Patrick.

"Maybe."

"Do you think Nancy's really in a spot, dear? Or was Gwennie just showing off in front of Phil?"

"In what way?"

"Phil likes Nancy, obviously. Maybe Gwen is showing him what a good friend she is to Nancy. Gwen's full of tricks."

"Might be."

"You certainly are helpful, Pat."

"Sorry."

The cab left us at our place, turned around on the flat circle guarded by a balustrade where Green Street suddenly becomes stair steps, and moved off.

We climbed the tiled stairs to the little front portico of the apartment house and Patrick opened the heavy grilled door. The building was neo-Spanish in a style popular about twenty years ago. We liked the building well enough, but disliked our furnished apartment on the fifth floor, because it was stuffily crowded with phony antiques and oriental art objects. But we didn't go on up just now. Vincent Smith, the night elevator man, and alone on the job now because of the labor shortage, stopped us as we headed for the cage.

"Hey, a lady came to see you," he said. His weasel eyes twisted with curiosity. "A Mrs. Leland. She says she lives on Jones Street and will you come over there at once because it's urgent." I could tell by his face that he knew about the murder. Nancy couldn't've mentioned it. It may have been in the late papers.

"Thanks, Vincent." To me, "Want to go?"

I could see that his apparent lack of interest bothered Vincent Smith. He looked disappointed.

I yawned, for Vincent's benefit. "I don't care. Might as well, maybe."

"Okay. Let's make it snappy."

"All right."

We nodded at Vincent and walked out. "He's heard the news," I said, as we trotted down the tiled steps.

"I guess so."

We walked quickly.

"I suppose Nancy has decided to take Gwen's advice," I said, about the time we got back to Jones Street.

Patrick pressed my arm for silence.

Padding steps sounded beyond the greenery on the corner. The man in the light raincoat we had seen standing opposite Nancy's house came into view. He slowed up. We crossed Jones in front of him and turned left toward Nancy's.

The man came to a dead halt and stood watching us as we walked up the easy incline. Then he followed. When we arrived at Nancy's gate he was about thirty steps behind.

My back crawled. I said, "He's not even trying to keep from being noticed."

"Probably that's his idea."

"You mean they want Nancy to think she's being watched?"

"Could be."

We opened the gate and walked along the flagged walk between rose trees which scented the air with their fragrance. The lawn was an oblong and a bright emerald in color by day, edged by hedges of a glistening evergreen plant I could never remember the name of. The drive into the garage which was attached by a passage to the house was separated from the lawn by one of these hedges, and another divided it from a rocky vacant lot next door. A lamp in the carriage style glowed on either side of the white-painted door. We rang and almost at once the door was opened by an exquisitely pretty Chinese girl with a permanent and a feather cut. I didn't recognize her for a moment as Rosalie Wong.

"You've grown up since we saw you!" I said then.

"I'm eighteen," she said, blushing. She had a voice like silver bells.

Rosalie took our things and laid them on a chair to the left of the door in the spacious fore part of the hall. A staircase with white balusters and a mahogany railing was straight ahead. We turned right toward the living room.

Rosalie wore a black uniform and a white apron. Patrick asked her about school. She was a sophomore at the university, she said. He said he supposed she would make honors like her sisters. She smiled and said she was trying hard. I asked after her mother, Mary Wong, the cook and housekeeper, whom we had not seen since coming back. Her mother had taken an extra job evenings, Rosalie said, which was why she herself was here. She could do her homework and be here if Miss Nancy needed her. I thought how proud Mary must be of this daughter when she started off to school each morning, dressed like any American girl in a skirt and sweater, a tweed coat, bobby socks and saddle oxfords. And she had six others besides Rosalie.

Rosalie opened the living-room door and spoke our names and waited to close the door after us.

Nancy Leland rose lightly from a sofa near an open fire and came toward us across the big wood-paneled room.

FIVE

Patrick thinks that all greatly attractive women have in their faces a hint of mystery. The first time I heard him say so I asked if that applied to me and he naturally said of course. I never could see it myself when I looked in the mirror, but of Nancy Leland it was indubitably true. You looked at Nancy, and then you looked again and again to single out her special appeal. Maybe you would dismiss it as charm. But it was that and more. It was the feeling that it would take time to know her well. It was the way her face lighted when she smiled. It was that suggestion of mystery.

That woman we had seen with the gray-haired man in that Mexican jive-joint had achieved a sort of mystery by her fine clothes and her silence and so on. But in Nancy Leland it was innate, because we knew her well and in all her moods and phases still there it was.

The living room had a thick green carpet, yellow flowered-chintz covers on the comfortable sofas and chairs, many books and magazines, a modern portable bar in one corner and beside it an old fashioned tea-table. Plain green curtains usually hung on either side of the venetian blinds fitted to the almost continuous windows along two sides of the big room.

When you walked into this room, there, through all those windows, was usually a vast portion of the harbor spreading before you, including the far brown hills, Mount Tamalpais, the Golden Gate, the blue depthless ocean beyond.

Tonight everything was different and rather spoiled because the slats of the blinds were closed and the heavy curtains were drawn until they made an almost continuous green wall.

Nancy was tall, as tall as I, with dark curling hair cut short and brushed off her triangular dark-eyed face. Her eyes were dark, and strikingly shaped. She had good, useful-looking hands and a pleasant voice. She wore a dark-brown tweed suit, a lime-green sweater, and a string of good artificial pearls.

Two sofas faced each other across the fireplace. I sat down away from the fire on the one where Nancy had been sitting. She resumed the same place after we had declined her offered drink. Patrick sat down facing her and started rolling one of his cigarettes.

"I'd offer you one if I had one," Nancy said. She seldom smoked. "I might as well get straight to the point before anybody comes," she said. "You're sure you won't have a drink? I've got some perfectly horrible bourbon, if you change your minds. I suppose that elevator man at your place delivered my message?" I said he had. "By the way, did you notice a man watching this house?"

Patrick nodded. Nancy smiled. Her eyebrows were fine, and very expressive of her moods. "I wasn't quite sure that he was," she said. "Frankly, the reason I walked over to see you instead of phoning was to test that man in the white raincoat. Sure enough, he followed me there and then he followed me back. What do you do in a case like that, Pat?"

"Nothing, Nancy."

"That man worries me, Pat."

"That may be why he's there."

Nancy sat up straight. "What a dirty trick!" she said. "But I knew it. When I first noticed the man hanging around I called up the police and talked with that Inspector who came here and asked me questions about Ernest. He thanked me for telling him about the man in the raincoat and said he would take care of it promptly. And of course he hasn't."

"Why have you got these blinds closed?" Patrick asked.

"Because that man gives me horrors."

"But no one can see into this room, unless with glasses from some other house," Patrick said. The house rested at the back and at this end on a rock. There was a drop of twenty feet beneath these windows to a garden below, which belonged to a house fronting on another street. Nancy's house was accessible only from Jones Street. Her garage adjoined the house, and its drive, parted, as I said, from the lawn by a shiny evergreen hedge, ran parallel with the flagged walk. The service entrance led from this drive into the passage which joined the garage to the house. On the second floor the upstairs portion of the passage connected the apartment used by Mary Wong.

Nancy said, "It's a waste of man-power, if nothing else."

"That's one of the troubles with murder. It wastes a lot of good time for everybody concerned. For other people, too."

Nancy looked grave. "But why suspect me?"

"Everybody intimately connected with Leland will be under suspicion till the murderer is isolated, Nancy. Particularly everyone who might profit by his death."

I said, "It would be easy for that plainclothes man to keep out of sight, the way the rocks and trees and bushes pile up on each other around here."

"They don't want him out of sight," Nancy said. "They want gradually to drive me crazy. And they're doing it. I can't tell you how he upsets me. It's un-American!" she declared. "It's not fair."

"It's also for your protection, perhaps," Patrick told her.

"Why on earth should I need protection?"

Patrick said, "If I could answer that, I would probably know who murdered your husband."

Nancy relaxed into the corner of the sofa. She spoke with a catch in her throat. "My husband. That's what I keep forgetting! That police detective kept calling Ernest my husband. He was, of course. Legally."

"Why hadn't you divorced him, Nancy?"

Nancy said, "I don't know. Oh, yes, I do. I just hated to go ahead and make the break final. Ernest was so decent. And every time I brought up the subject he asked me please to wait just a little while longer—and I was working, of course, six days a week, without a minute really to call my own—and there wasn't any real rush. It wasn't as though he made things difficult." She pushed her black up-curling hair back from her wide forehead. "Pat, there's something I am not going to tell the police and that's that Ernest called me on the phone last night and said he had to see me at once. It was after midnight. He said he was in town only for a few hours and he wanted to talk to me about the divorce. He asked me on the phone if I would go to Reno. I said I didn't want to because I would have to leave my defense job for six weeks. He reminded me it took a full year to get a final decree in California. I asked him if he wanted to marry again, meaning to go to Reno if that was his reason, and he hesitated and then said he didn't want to talk any more about it on the phone and could he come here. It occurred to me that it was peculiar in Ernest to have called me on the phone about anything so personal. He was usually very reticent about private affairs. Also there must have been somebody he was afraid was overhearing the conversation because he muffled his voice when he asked to come. I thought afterwards, when he never showed up, that maybe I hadn't understood exactly what he said."

"You say you didn't tell the police inspector you expected Ernest here last night?"

"No. I'm not going to tell it."

"Why not?"

"I can't," Nancy said.

"Are you protecting someone?"

"Of course not," Nancy said.

"No one else knew he was coming here to see you?"

"I don't know. As I said, I had that feeling that somebody was listening. Of course, he might have phoned from a hotel. You know how the phone sounds sometimes when a call comes through an extra switchboard, I mean as though somebody was eavesdropping or maybe he was with somebody and being careful."

"Leland much of a lady's man?" Patrick asked.

Nancy flushed. "I don't think so, Pat. No, I'd say. He seemed entirely wound up in his business. He was obsessed with it." She said, with a crooked smile, "I don't really know why he ever took time to get married and have a wife. I bored him. I always had a feeling that he allowed me only a fraction of his attention, and that for only a few minutes now and then. This house bored him to death. Home life seemed to be a waste of his time. That, frankly, was why we separated. He liked his hotel life. It was more efficient. And I couldn't endure it after the glamour wore off. I was miserable and he was, too, if he had only taken time to think it out!"

"He was a good deal older than you, wasn't he?"

"Maybe that was the trouble."

"Why did you marry him, really?"

Nancy answered at once.

"I adored him. My father died and I was lonely and Ernest seemed the answer."

"Known him long?"

"Not when we married. I met him through Rufus. You both know my brother Rufus. He had a job with the Leland interests in Southern California. It seems that Ernest had invested in all kinds of things down that way and there's an office in Los Angeles where everything clears. Rufus is now in charge there. Six months after father died I went to stay a while with Rufus and Helen—you haven't met Rufus's wife, they were married about a year before Ernest and me—well, anyway, I met him down there, even though what he called his home was up here, and in six weeks we married. Rufus and Helen are in town, by the way. They phoned just before you arrived and will be along soon."

"Does anyone know he telephoned you last night?"

"Nobody but Gwen Telfer. I told Gwen, before I thought."

"Did you know when you married Leland about his previous marriage?" Patrick asked.

"Oh, yes. His wife died before I met him. They'd been separated for many years."

"Nancy—was he vindictive?"

There was a distinct pause.

"No."

"You knew he had a son?"

Nancy nodded her dark head. "Yes. By the way, did Gwen Telfer get in touch with you, by any chance?"

"We had dinner with her."

Nancy put her hands together; her fingers began a nervous sort of twisting. "Gwen's crazy," she said. "She insists that I am in danger, that I ought to get a lawyer or a detective or somebody to handle this for me. Why? I don't need help. I'm not guilty of anything. I think all I need to do is answer their questions and just wait. It's ridiculous for people to get all hot and bothered on my account, like Gwen. It's nice of her to want you to help me, but it's silly."

Patrick said, "Gwen has a practical viewpoint. She probably senses what the police will think better than you do, Nancy. They will consider—whether true or not—that there was bad feeling between you and Leland because you were separated. If they find out that he came to ask you for a divorce, in the middle of the night like that, they will insist there is another woman, and if the papers get it you know what *that* means. If you come into his property it's not going to help, either."

"Well, maybe I won't. Or maybe I can give it away."

"Maybe. But you can't give it away or anything else till you are cleared of a charge of murder. Assuming it is made, of course. I don't want to scare you, Nancy. I'm just warning you of what can happen."

Nancy kept twisting her fingers.

"Did Inspector Bradish tell you Ernest was killed with cyanide?" Patrick asked.

"Yes." Her lips curved bitterly. "He did, and he asked me if it was easy to get where I work, and I told him it was, if anyone happened to want it. Anybody there could tell him the same."

Patrick asked, "Do you think there was possibility of suicide?"

Nancy seemed almost startled.

"No!"

"You seem very positive, Nancy."

"If you had known him you would say the same thing. He was so interested in his business affairs, his schemes." Nancy smiled and her face came alight. "He wouldn't have killed himself for fear he might miss something." She leaned toward Patrick, and asked softly, "Pat, would it be irregular or something if you just *pretended* to be working for me on this case? I would pay you just the same."

Patrick smiled.

"I'm afraid that would suit me very well indeed. Except that I couldn't possibly accept the fee."

Nancy sat back against the sofa and stared at him.

"In the first place, as I would have told Gwen had she persisted in demanding my services for you, I really haven't got time now for any more work than I've already got lined up. Gwen rather took it for granted that I would jump at this case."

Nancy sat forward.

"Look here, Pat, I want to pay you just the same. Even though you are only pretending to be working for me."

"Skip it, Nancy. But why do you want it that way?"

Nancy smiled all over her face.

"I want Gwen Telfer to lay off me and let things take their natural course. That's all I want. Gwen makes me—well, a little weary. You know how she is. She thinks she knows what is best for everybody and half the time she doesn't know it at all. I'll admit she's a whiz in business. But people are something else. Gwen is always talking about how she understands people and she doesn't at all."

"If I may say so," I said, "you're dead right, Nancy."

"I guess you both think I'm nuts, though," Nancy said.

"I think you're very sweet," Patrick said. Tears suddenly came into Nancy's dark eyes. "I always have. By the way, there is something else you ought to know. Jean and I saw Leland's car wrecked last night. I didn't go down to the scene of the wreck for about twenty minutes—there was a thick fog up here on the hill and I took Jean home first—and then even when I got back to the wreck I didn't know the dead man was Ernest Leland. But Inspector Bradish is very suspicious of me, Nancy. So if I started being your private investigator there'd be hell to pay. He already thinks I ran up here last night after seeing the wreck to warn you to lie low, and along with it to get myself a nice fat job of work saving your young neck."

"But how on earth?" Nancy gasped.

"Because Bradish started working backward from a post mortem. He knows to start with that Leland was murdered before the car was wrecked. He knows you're an old friend of ours. He guesses you are coming into big money. He imagines I dashed up here to get in ahead of the police—and being a practical fellow himself I wouldn't be surprised if he doesn't believe that I put the money I'd expect to get paid ahead of our old friendship."

"For heaven's sake!" Nancy said. "Did you tell Gwen all that?"

"He didn't have a chance," I said. "Gwen did practically all the talking, till Phil Hannegan stopped her . . ."

"Phil Hannegan?" Nancy said, and she sat back against the back of the sofa again and tried too abruptly to look diffident.

"Phil thought Gwen was making a mistake," Patrick said. "By the way, Nancy, what about that hat?"

"Hat?"

"Bradish tells me your hat was found in Leland's car. A rose-colored feather hat."

Several expressions followed each other across Nancy Leland's mobile face. It paled, it looked glazed, it turned pink, and it became rather sullen-looking.

And she made no comment on the hat, for at that moment a bell sounded distantly and saying that it must be Rufus and Helen she excused herself quickly and hurried to meet them at the door. We heard them greeting each other warmly in the hall, and then Rufus Moore came into the room, a little ahead of the two girls. He was a solid-looking, pink-cheeked man, of middle height, and he wore a navy chalk-striped suit. He had protuberant light-brown eyes, a short and rather fleshy nose, and a well-shaped mouth with teeth which were his best feature and, when he smiled, improved his appearance very much. When he didn't smile you didn't like his face. He moved with a great display of vitality. He thrust his arm out to shake hands the moment he entered the door.

We were shaking hands with Rufus when his wife came in with Nancy Leland. At the sight of her my heart started beating almost painfully, for Helen Moore, Rufus's wife, was the still-eyed woman in the costly minks we had seen with that distinguished-looking, desperate, pleading man in that Mexican joint last night.

SIX

Rufus wanted a drink. He had a fifth of good Scotch in his bag, he said, when Nancy mentioned the low quality of her only whisky, the bourbon. "Ring for that girl and get some ice," he said. Already he was striding out of the room. We had got settled, Helen Moore on the sofa with me, Nancy on the other one with Patrick, and Rufus had pulled up a wing-chair in which he had not yet sat down.

As he left the room the light glinted for a moment on a small bald spot on the crown of his head. It looked strangely vulnerable, a spot of weakness in a man who otherwise looked so determined in his thick phlegmatic way that I quailed at the very thought of Nancy's having to explain something out of the ordinary to him.

Nancy rang for Rosalie and asked Helen what kind of trip they had had. Helen—in a smart gray-flannel dress, her gilt-yellow hair as carefully arranged as though she had only walked across the street, her minks over her shoulders until, as she had said on coming in, she got over feeling chilled—said it hadn't been bad. "I hate flying, however, and I've had so much of it the past twenty-four hours I'm dizzy, Nancy. My mother is very ill, in San Diego. I flew down to see her last night and had just got home when Rufus telephoned me the terrible news about Ernest."

What a whopper, I thought. She had been here, right in San Francisco, last night. The dress was different, but there were those minks, and there on her left hand was the wedding ring and the medium-sized diamond which Patrick had cracked had been acquired when her husband—that distinguished gray-haired man—had less money than now.

Her husband! Unless she had two on her hands something was very haywire. But, of course, last night we had been guessing about her just for fun.

Those were her hands, dead-white hands with the long, tended nails enameled the color of old blood.

Yet her face was somehow different. She had a wonderful smile and lovely teeth. Her eyes were not so still-looking. They looked, as she spoke with Nancy, almost demure. Her voice, which we hadn't heard last night, was rather ordinary, had a flat thin texture which was not up to her looks. She was in a sense a beautiful woman. But she lacked Gwendolyn Telfer's magnetic fire and individuality, and she was without Nancy Leland's dark-eyed plastic charm.

"Is your mother very seriously ill, Helen?" Nancy asked.

The woman's face shadowed. "She won't get well."

"I'm so sorry."

Helen said, "She suffers so much that you sometimes wish the doctors wouldn't keep working to prolong her life. I'm—I'm so fond of her. She did everything in the world for me, Nancy. Simply everything. I feel like a cheat because I never achieved what she hoped for and worked for."

I looked at Patrick. My curiosity about this woman was certainly in my gaze because it positively made butterflies flit about my middle. If her mother was really mortally ill and she could sit here and lie about being with her last night, something ought really to strike her dead.

Pat did not return my glance. He was listening to Helen with the utmost gravity, his long eyes devoid of any expression save sympathy. Didn't he remember her then? I'd been a lot more fascinated by that couple than Pat was. He listened as Helen told her young sister-in-law about her hurried trip to San Diego, her return to her home in Los Angeles this morning, and their luck in getting plane accommodations to San Francisco.

"I barely had time to change my dress," she said.

Rosalie had fetched the ice-cubes in a bucket and had wheeled the portable bar beside Rufus's chair by the time he came back. One of his rather clumsy-looking hands clutched a bottle of Vat-69. He asked us to say when, and served up the whisky to our individual tastes.

Every movement of his big well-turned-out body advertised his upset mind. But his pale bulging eyes never changed.

He sat down at last in the chair. He leaned forward and spoke to Patrick.

"I'm glad you've taken this case, Pat. But we also need a lawyer. Anybody in a fix needs a good lawyer. There's no time to lose. I'd like to get the facts straight at once and then call the lawyer. Gwen Telfer has recommended the right man. I respect her judgment."

"Gwen?" Nancy snapped. "Well, for heaven's sake!"

"Gwen knows what she's talking about, sister."

"The hell with Gwen," Nancy said.

"Now don't take that attitude," Rufus said, with a show of impatience. Then he said, "Look here, are you alone in the house these nights?"

Nancy shook her head.

"Mary is here. Sometimes Rosalie, too."

"Where's Mary tonight?"

Nancy said, "She's got two jobs now. She could earn so much extra working evenings now at a café in Chinatown that I urged her to do it. She's in debt, Rufus. It costs money to send seven girls to college, even when you keep nothing for yourself."

"They ought to be supporting her by this time," Rufus said.

"She won't have it. They've been educated for the New China, and that's where they'll go. Four have gone out there already, as Wacs. Two are working in defense plants and parking their money to go out to China when the war's ended. There's a future for American-educated Chinese."

Rufus listened. With impatience.

"Were you alone here last night when—at the time Ernest was murdered?"

Nancy frowned hard. "Who told you he was murdered?"

"We stopped to see Gwen. I thought you would know that, Nancy. On our way from the airport."

Nancy's hands started working again.

"You might have had the good manners to hear my side of the story first, Rufus."

Rufus's square chin became a knot.

"Now, listen. There's no other side, so far as I know. Gwen called me long distance and said there were things she must tell me that she couldn't tell over the phone, and she suggested that I stop at her apartment as soon as I got in. It was the time to see Gwen. This house is under police surveillance. I may not be free to come and go as I like. And I didn't know until I saw Gwen that Ernest had been murdered. I knew he was dead—accidentally, I thought—but *murdered*! My word, I'm upset!"

There was a silence.

"It's terrible for Helen, too," he said. "She'd known Ernest longer than any of us."

Helen gave her husband a soft glance and said nothing.

"Well, we needn't go into that at a time like this," he said then. "Were Mary and Rosalie here in the house last night? I mean, at the time he was murdered?"

"I really have no idea," Nancy said, almost flippantly, too.

Patrick was silent and attentive. He could be such a good listener that souls were always being bared to him—and like as not his time wasted.

Rufus began talking to Patrick specially, his prominent eyes fixed and staring.

"There's not a chance of suicide, Pat. Ernest would never do it."

"You think not?" Patrick said.

"Never. He wasn't the type." Rufus got up and began to stride around the room, his steps padding softly on the thick green carpet. He talked as he walked. "He wasn't ill. He wasn't old, just past forty. He was terribly pleased about some new deal he'd just pulled off in Old Mexico. When he called me from the airport in L.A. yesterday afternoon he told me he couldn't tell me the details in the short time he had—he'd chartered a plane and it had to take off at once—but he'd fly up here and come back down in a day or two and give me all the dope. I wanted him to stop over, but he said he had to get up here pronto to see Nancy."

"To see me?" Nancy said. "I didn't even know he was due back."

"He told me he was dying to see you. He somehow gave me the idea there was to be a reconciliation. He sounded—well, jubilant."

"There was to be nothing of the kind!" Nancy said.

Rufus stopped beside the mantelpiece and set his high-ball glass upon it with a sharp click.

"Don't tell that to the police, Nancy."

"Why not? It isn't so. I never, at any time . . ."

"All right! All right! But use a little sense. I want you to tell the lawyer Gwen has picked out for us that you and Ernest were patching things up, that you were calling off divorce proceedings . . ."

"But that's not true," Nancy said.

Rufus said with phlegmatic patience, "I talked it over with Gwen, dear. It's the only way. If you don't take advice and follow it you'll—you'd end up in the gas chamber at San Quentin." Nancy sniffed. "I'm sorry to be brutal, dear, but I must be. You've got to face the facts. Leland phoned you last night after he got in and came up here to see you and the next thing anybody knows he was dead. You inherit. Thanks to Gwen Telfer we have inside information on his will. You haven't got a leg to stand on, Nancy. You haven't even got an alibi."

"How do you know I haven't got an alibi?" Nancy muttered stubbornly.

"You were evidently alone in this house at the time Ernest was murdered. Mary Wong's being in the garage apartment won't help you much unless . . ."

"Oh, so what!" Nancy said. "My goodness!"

Rufus kept his patience.

"I went over every angle with Gwen. That's why we were so long getting here. I would have brought her lawyer here with me but he has gone to Sacramento and can't be reached till after midnight." All at once Rufus Moore struck the mantel with his clenched fist. "What on earth possessed you to leave Ernest Leland, Nancy? There isn't a better man on this earth."

Nancy said slowly, "If Ernest had given a damn whether I left him or not, that might have mattered some, Rufus."

"Don't be silly! He adored you with all his heart!"

"All he had," Nancy said.

"He was absolutely devoted to you!"

"Nuts! I took too much of his valuable time," said Nancy.

Rufus reddened. "He was generous to a fault."

"I never said he wasn't. When it came to money. But just try to claim a few minutes of his priceless time. Unless he was in the mood, which wasn't often, I can tell you."

"You had no real cause to divorce him," Rufus said obstinately. "If you wouldn't consider yourself you might have considered me."

"You?" Nancy cried.

"Us, I should have said. You know perfectly well that I owe my present job and my present salary to Ernest Leland. Not only I, but my wife, are completely dependent on your whims."

"Whims?"

Rufus Moore expanded his ample chest with a long in-drawn breath. "I'm sorry to drag out the family skeleton with the Abbotts present...."

"They should be present, darling," Helen Moore said unexpectedly, her flat voice softening as she addressed her husband. "After all, Mr. Abbott is working for us."

Us? Without looking at her I saw her, last night, sitting like a rock in that café. The poor man pleaded. She never yielded one inch. And Pat had opined that they were married! That he would kiss her in the taxi! Buy her a diamond necklace. In a horrid sort of way it made a kind of sense. Maybe they weren't married but maybe there was a kiss in a taxi and—more minks.

"You knew Leland very well, didn't you, Rufus?" Patrick asked.

"I've worked for him for several years. I even met my wife through Ernest Leland. I knew him in business and I knew him as a personal friend and relation. They don't come any better, Pat. He was generous with everybody who worked for him. I would stand up and swear on a stack of Bibles that he hadn't an enemy in all the world."

"Was he ever vindictive?"

"Vindictive?" Rufus shouted. "Good God, no!"

"You knew he had been married before?"

"Yes, of course. His first wife died before he met Nancy. He supported their boy, sent him to the best schools in the East."

"Did he support his former wife?"

"She didn't want it. She had money of her own."

"You are sure of all this, I suppose?"

"Of course. After all, even though he was my boss he was going to marry my little sister, so I took a good deal of pains to find out all about him. That is, all I didn't already know. He would probably have fired me if he had known how many questions I asked about him behind his back."

"Have you seen his son?" Patrick asked.

There was a slight tension in Rufus's manner. Helen Moore did not change. She was sitting quietly, as she had been all along.

"No, I haven't. I understand he came out here and threatened to kill his father. Gwen advises that we not discuss that. She says Chris Leland is the ace up our sleeve. But maybe we'd better lead with the ace, Pat. With your permission—I know you know more about this sort of thing than I do—I'd like to get together with the police, and have that boy rounded up and popped into jail."

"Jail?" Nancy said. "Why?"

"Because he came out here to murder his father and his father straight away got murdered. That boy must be arrested, even if only on suspicion. It will at least remove suspicion from you, sister. If he murdered his father no doubt the police will know how to make him confess. If he didn't, it will teach him a lesson."

Nancy smiled an odd smile. "Do you yourself suspect me of killing Ernest, Rufus?"

There was a short and strangely embarrassing silence. Rufus looked into the fire. He fumbled at the glass in which the ice had melted as he clasped it warmly off and on the mantelpiece. He cleared his throat. Nancy sat watching him. Her eyes began to shine with a slow fine malice.

"Now, look here, sis," he said finally, "I'm a lot older than you are and I know a lot more about human nature than you ever will probably. Somebody has to take the rap . . ."

"So we'll be big and noble and let Chris Leland take it," Nancy said.

"Oh, I don't mean permanently, dear. I mean, let them chuck the kid in jail for a while, won't hurt him, and meanwhile the excitement will die down. He's better off in jail anyway if he hasn't any better sense than to run around with a gun telling people he's going to kill his father. Naturally I don't want him executed, if he's innocent. Which I doubt."

"I see," Nancy said.

Rufus fidgeted, then said, "Ring for more ice, will you, Nancy? Here, I'll do it."

There was a push button near the mantel. The late Mr. Moore had been very long an invalid and much had been done to make him comfortable. There were push buttons all over the house, and sockets in which to plug special lights, and others for portable telephones.

"Nancy, dear, I want to tell you a story," Rufus said, and with a kind of blurting tenderness. "I know a man whose wife was murdered shortly after their marriage. The murder was never solved. Because of the scandal he lost his job. When the police stopped bothering him he got another, and since he was smart he did all right. But the news followed him around. Somebody in the business he was in stole a lot of money and right away he was suspected. He was proved innocent, but the old scandal was revived. The thief was found, but somehow suspicion hung over the poor guy and he finally resigned. That time he went out and bought a ranch. It does all right. He got married again and has some children—but nobody ever mentions him that it isn't also mentioned that he was once suspected of doing murder." There was a longish silence. "Nancy—I hope you understand now why we've got to clap Chris Leland into jail!"

Nancy began to laugh hysterically. "You mean," she squeaked through her crazy laughter, "to keep the cloud from hanging over me? But what about Chris? Won't the same sort of thing happen to him?"

"All right. Call a spade a spade. This was certainly a deliberated murder. It was planned. Maybe you wrote to Ernest, asked him to come, promised to go back to him, or this or that. Maybe you have involved yourself more than you realize."

He broke off. Mary Wong entered the door at the far end of the room which opened into the service hall.

In her plain black dress, with a hastily tied-on white apron, the Chinese woman looked smaller and older than she actually was. Her black straight hair was drawn straight away from her yellow seamed face. Yet she had a kind of beauty, in her expression, the kindliness of her eyes, in her dignity, and in the gentle-mannered greetings she gave us.

"Rosalie has gone to her room to work on her lessons, Miss Nancy. You did ring?" She spoke with a flat cracked voice that had none of the silver-bell character of her daughter's.

Rufus answered. "More ice cubes, Mary. You might rustle up a few sandwiches or something, too, for Mrs. Moore and me. We didn't get any dinner."

"Perhaps you would like ham and eggs, Mr. Rufus?"

"Yes, thank you, Mary," Helen Moore said, with her sweet smile.

Mary Wong left the room.

Rufus said, "Does Mary know about Ernest, Nancy?"

"Yes. I told her. He came here to live for a few weeks, as you know, after I got so I couldn't stand living in hotels any longer. Mary liked him very much, I think. He was always very considerate and, as you said, very generous with money."

"We want to make sure she is on our side," Rufus said.

Nancy laughed, again bitterly. "You sound as if we're running for office, or something. Mary will tell the truth, I hope. What she knows of it. Precious little, I think."

"Let's stop this bickering, sister," Rufus said, in a gentler tone. He was still standing by the fireplace. "You know Mary. You know she will say just exactly what she is coached to say. She's that loyal. Now, another thing, what about that hat that was found in Ernest's car?"

Nancy's voice was barely audible.

"Have you already been interviewed by the police, Rufus?"

"No."

"Then how did you know about the hat?"

"Gwen told me. Who else?"

"*And how did Gwen know that hat was in the wrecked car?*"

"Well, what is so mysterious about the hat? Besides, you took Gwen into your full confidence. . . ."

Nancy laughed quietly, in her throat.

"Gwen is the last person on earth I would have mentioned that hat to, Rufus."

"Well, forget that, now." Mary had come back with the ice. Rufus went around to the little bar. "Say when, everybody."

Patrick and I declined a second drink. Patrick said we had to be moving. Rufus left the bar temporarily and asked what we would be doing about the case yet tonight. Patrick replied vaguely that he would do whatever was indicated. We shook hands with Rufus, exchanged polite nods with Helen Moore, and Nancy came with us to the front door.

In the hall she said, "Don't let Rufus get you upset, Pat. He always gets hot and bothered about anything to start with. Helen will calm him down."

"Tell me something, Nancy," Patrick said. "Are you and Phil in love?"

Blushes covered Nancy's face, making it very lovely.

"Why, Pat! What an idea!"

"Just be careful, child. That's all."

As we left the house I saw a tall figure slip away from the sidewalk and hide behind a patch of flowering broom to the left of the entrance. I supposed it was a plainclothes man. I felt uncomfortable, and I slipped an arm tightly through Patrick's as we walked away along the walk. There was something much more important than that figure to talk about now. I said it in a whisper, near the gate.

"Pat, didn't you recognize her? Helen Moore is that babe we saw with that fine-looking man in that Mexican dive last night. Remember?"

Patrick answered under his breath.

"The man," he said, "was Ernest Leland."

SEVEN

In vast patches the fog had come in from the sea and had started creeping over the hill while we sat in Nancy's living room. It felt cold and damp. It was full of great holes between patches in which you could see the stars far above in a black, cloud-edged sky. As we walked we noticed high up through one of these wells in the fog a navy blimp patrolling the bay. Its aluminum paint reflected the light of a moon which, even if the night had been clear, would not shine on this hill for several hours. The fog extended tonight down to the level of the water. We could hear the foghorn moaning on Alcatraz.

I felt frightened. I clung to Patrick's arm, dying to ask questions which must not be voiced till we were in the privacy of our own walls. And I could hear footsteps following us. The footfalls of the man who had rushed undercover as we left Nancy's house? Perhaps. I remembered for no particular reason that the bush which gave him that sudden shelter was filled by day with masses of yellow flowers.

So the woman in the Mexican nightclub had been Helen Moore. And that distinguished-looking, worried man was Ernest Leland.

He had been murdered within a short time, hardly an hour, after he left that dive.

The woman left the dive with him.

They had been quarreling.

Would you call it a quarrel? He had been pleading. She had been mulelike in her refusal to do whatever it was he wanted. Perhaps a quarrel had occurred before they came in and her wall of silence was her grand finale at whipping him into line. What was it she had wanted?

Ernest Leland had come by private plane from Los Angeles last night. An unidentified woman had accompanied him. It didn't take much ingenuity to figure out now that that woman was Helen Moore.

What did Patrick think?

This was no time to ask that. For those footsteps kept trailing us in the fog.

Just when had Leland telephoned Nancy last night? That must have happened shortly after they left the Mexican place. He had said, over the phone, that he wanted to talk about the divorce. He had said he was willing to let it go ahead. He had put it off a long time, had even bucked it—and then, suddenly, in the middle of the night, he had phoned Nancy that he must see her at once to make plans for a divorce.

Was that what Helen Moore had demanded from him last night?

Had Leland given in because she forced it? Why? Had she stayed with him until he telephoned Nancy that he wanted to settle the business straight off? Had Helen come with him up to Russian Hill to make sure he didn't run out on her? And then, if he balked, had she polished him off with a hypo loaded with potassium cyanide? And then started the car down the hill? Did Rufus know all about it? Was it his wife Rufus was trying to protect more even than his sister?

Or was Rufus Moore merely fighting to hang onto his own job? Trying to prevent a scandal which involved his family, even if an innocent boy took the rap? Anything so long as his own excellent job was not jeopardized? Was that it?

I conjured up his square face, the pale-brown eyes, the thick nose, the good-looking mouth which didn't smile often enough. That face seemed thickly insensitive. It had softened only when he turned to his wife. Nancy had said their marriage was a happy one. That she was glad, because—for her sake and her father's—he had been kept from marrying while young. Had Nancy said that because she knew something about Helen that she was anxious that Rufus shouldn't find out?

Did Nancy know in some mysterious fashion that we had accidentally seen Helen Moore with Ernest Leland in the nightclub?

Or was there an affair between Ernest Leland and Helen Moore? *Would that explain Nancy's leaving Ernest Leland after only six months of marriage? Was that the true cause?* She probably hadn't fallen in love with Philip Hannegan before she left Leland, because at that time Philip was in the war. She had known Philip a long time, of course, but people often fall in love suddenly with people they've long known well.

I had taken a violent dislike to Helen Moore. Who wouldn't? A woman who one evening could be that bitchy still-eyed creature and the next such a devoted-seeming wife.

We had got to the intersection of Jones and Green Streets. Here the fog lay thick and consolidated. It went straight to the bone and was cold as a knife. A street lamp was a dim form topped by an opaline blur. We slowed down and walked with caution. Visibility was only a few feet. It had been even worse last night, though, when that car had plunged down this hill. The car had moved along softly down the incline we had just covered until it reached this spot. Here it had hesitated, briefly. Why?

Had it been guided as far as this point? Had the one who guided it stepped out here at this leveled intersection, and then let the car run on wildly down the steep portion of the hill? No door had stood open when we saw it, but the pressure of air would keep it closed. Who had done it? Helen Moore? Helen Moore had been with Ernest Leland last night. She had come with him from Los Angeles. To alibi herself she had told that whopper about being with her mother in San Diego. Rufus probably knew better. Maybe Nancy knew better. Maybe even Gwen Telfer did, too.

But what about the hat in the car? It was Nancy's shocking pink hat.

All at once Patrick gripped my arm and pulled us up short. Almost instantly footsteps following us also stopped. Such as we did hear were nervous, and cautious.

We stood listening. All was silence, save the faraway sounds in the fog, the hum of traffic, the reiterant moaning of the foghorn.

We turned into Green Street.

After a few steps Patrick whirled me about suddenly and we dashed back a few paces the way we had come.

A moving blur halted, and then crouched and then turned and receded, running away on panicky scrambling feet.

I began to shake like a leaf. My teeth chattered.

"It's the same as last night," I said.

Patrick put his arm about me, and, turning us again, walked us along to the apartment house.

Thin, weasel-faced Vincent Smith rose as we entered from a carved oak garnet-velvet upholstered chair designed in olden times for a king. His pointed eyes took on a crafty look as he followed us into the elevator cage.

"Lot of people looking for you tonight," he said. He closed the grill and started the cage upward. "A big man I guess is a plainclothes man wanted to know where you were, but I didn't tell him, see. A funny-looking kid with red hair came in once and wanted you, and then kept dodging around outside in the fog. Your telephone kept ringing, a lot."

We were rising slowly upward.

"Can you hear our phone all the way to the lobby?" Patrick asked.

"Nope. I noticed it, when passing up and down."

"You've got good hearing, Vincent."

"Yep," Vincent said. He took it as a compliment. "There's lots of bad characters hanging round Frisco nowadays. I reckon I ought to carry a gun. The owner won't let me, though."

"I expect he knows you're capable of handling almost any situation without a gun, Vincent."

The cage took a cheerful spurt, because of the compliment.

"Well, I do my best. People don't appreciate it, though. They complain all the time. You can't be everywhere at once."

"You've got something there," Patrick said.

"But how many people knows that, Mr. Abbott?"

"Not many," Patrick said sympathetically. We had got to our floor. Patrick let me go out and handed Vincent Smith a silver dollar. It irked me, a good dollar forked out to such a worm. We walked along the tiled corridor and Patrick unlocked our front door and went ahead of me through the little foyer into the hall of the apartment.

I followed him, feeling the slight recoil I always had on returning to this place which neither smelled nor looked nor felt like home.

Patrick threw his coat and hat at a chair in the hall and headed on back toward the kitchen. I dropped my coat next his. As I walked along after Patrick I had a curious feeling of something left undone.

The telephone rang.

The bell was in the hall near the entrance, but there were connections for the phones around the apartment. Snapping on the lights Patrick took the call in the big white kitchen. The phone was plugged in next the table in the dinette. I hurried over beside Patrick, to hear what was said.

"Pat? Sam Bradish speaking. What were you doing at Nancy Leland's tonight?"

"Talking to Nancy. Sorry we were out when you called, Sam."

"I didn't leave my name," Bradish snapped.

"Why didn't you come on over to Mrs. Leland's, Sam?"

"I've got my reasons, Pat. Now, see here, you've got to lay off that case, see? I'm giving you fair warning. If you start working for Nancy Leland . . ."

"Oh, keep your shirt on, Sam. I'm not working for Nancy Leland."

"Then why did you go there?"

"She asked us. She was worried because you had a man watching her house. She called you about the same thing."

Bradish took breath. "That's right. But this happens to be murder."

"If you don't want people to see her why don't you arrest her and put her in jail?"

"It's certain people I object to, Pat."

"You mean, you haven't got enough evidence?"

"See here! That's not all. I'm up to my ears in something else. That doesn't mean we're not covering the Leland case. We've checked up on everybody that might have any connection with the case. We haven't interviewed Rufus Moore and his wife yet but evidently they're in the clear. I want to do that myself, anyway, and I can't get to it tonight. An operative in San Diego says that Mrs. Moore spent the night down there with her mother. Rufus Moore put his car into his garage a little after eight o'clock and got it out at the usual time this morning to go to his office. Evidently he can prove that he spent the night at home. That Chinese woman left the restaurant where she works at ten minutes past one in the morning. She couldn't have walked up to the Leland house in ten minutes. Or rather in five minutes, for you've got to allow a few minutes for the murder to be done and the car to be started down the hill. We know the car crashed at one-twenty. It's not going to hurt to lie low for a day or two, specially when a much more important pot I've been watching a long time is just about to boil. I've got another murder on my hands that's a lot more important than Ernest K. Leland's, even though the victim is somebody nobody ever heard of."

"Who is it, Sam?"

"Nobody anybody ever heard of, as I said." Bradish added bitterly, "The worst of it is that the Feds will get all the credit."

"If you're that busy you didn't come up here tonight just to tell me to stay away from Nancy Leland, did you, Sam?"

"This other murder was reported while I was up there. I didn't come there just to ask you to stay away from the suspect. I came to ask a few more questions about the Moore family."

"Well, Mrs. Leland's no client of mine, Sam. So stop worrying."

"Okay. But take it easy, Pat."

"Okay." Patrick cradled the receiver. "Let's cook bacon and eggs," he said. "The fog and that Scotch made me hungry."

Patrick appointed himself cook and I washed my hands and started setting the table. Once again I remembered there was something I had left undone, but I still couldn't think what it was. Maybe I had left something at Nancy's. Getting out the dishes for the table of the built-in dinette I asked Patrick what he thought about Bradish's saying that Helen Moore had spent last night with her mother in San Diego.

"Somebody apparently lied," he said.

"You didn't tell him she didn't, dear."

"No. Not yet."

"Why not?"

Patrick said, "What Rufus said about being suspected is true. Maybe none of them had anything to do with it. Maybe Gwen's right, maybe it was the kid, Chris Leland. Maybe it was none of them. No need to have the taint of suspicion hanging over the family if they're innocent."

"She's not entirely innocent," I said.

"Maybe not. But whatever involves her involves them all. There's got to be some other way to get at her, Jean."

"We could prove she was here, by that waiter in that dive, maybe."

Patrick was putting on the coffee. "He didn't look like a very good witness," he said. "But I'll trot down the steps and talk to him, just in case."

"I won't go with you if you're going to use the steps."

"They'll save time, Jeanie."

"Pat, why didn't you tell me that dead man was Ernest Leland?"

"I told you why. I didn't know it, till Bradish told me."

"Well, you certainly did know, as soon as you saw him in the wreck, that he was the man we had seen in that dive."

"Sure." Patrick was getting the bacon from the icebox.

"Well, why didn't you tell me that?"

"I didn't think, at that time, that it concerned us or anyone we knew. I didn't know the woman was Helen Moore."

He started laying out the slices of bacon in the heated iron skillet. I fetched the cream, sugar and butter.

"Then you really didn't go to see Nancy when you ran after that person in the fog?"

Patrick stood with an egg poised in one hand. "Hey?"

I said, "Well, the way you just handled Bradish on the phone—and you didn't tell me the man in the wreck was the one in the dive, so . . . ."

"You aren't Bradish, darling. Whenever I can, I tell you the truth, and all the truth. I didn't go to Nancy's after we saw the car wrecked. I didn't know then who Leland was. I was as surprised as you were when Helen Moore walked into that room tonight, and I recognized her from last night. Maybe I was much more surprised than you were, because I knew when I saw her tonight that she had been with Leland last night just before he was murdered—you didn't know, until I told you, that the gray-haired man in the dive was Leland. You only knew that she was the woman with the gray-haired man, and that she was lying about going to San Diego last night."

I nodded. Patrick broke the egg and dropped it in with the bacon. I fetched the toaster and some of the rye bread Patrick likes best. I opened a jar of strawberry preserves.

"Do you think she remembered us, Pat?"

"I—don't—know."

"Do you think Nancy knew Helen was up here last night with Leland?"

"I can't answer that, either."

"Nancy knows more than she let on," I said.

"Could be."

"There's the hat...."

"Yeah," Patrick said, breaking another egg into the skillet.

"Darling, don't you think you ought to ask Nancy some point-blank questions, and..."

"Nancy is not my client," Patrick said, taking out some crisply fried bacon and dropping in two more eggs. The delicious smell filled the kitchen. I hadn't thought I was hungry until now. I plugged in the toaster and put in two slices of bread to toast.

"Who followed us in the fog, Pat?"

"I don't know."

"It couldn't've been Bradish's man because I saw him dash behind a bush just as we came out of Nancy's door."

Patrick was busy with the spatula. He said, "The man who dashed behind that bush was Phil Hannegan."

"Darling?"

"The darn fool!" Patrick said indignantly. "He ought to have more sense. What possessed him to go there tonight? Maybe he thought the fog would hide him. If Nancy were my client—but, of course, she isn't."

Irrelevantly, that sense of something forgotten came back, and again I put it out of my mind.

"That must have been Chris Leland who came to see you tonight, Pat. Vincent Smith said a kid, and a redhead. I wonder why he came here?"

"Maybe Gwen changed her mind and sent Chris to be our client, Jeanie."

"Now don't make jokes, Pat." I turned the toast. "And take Gwen. She's another funny angle in this case. Here, there, everywhere—that's Gwen. Even Rufus and Helen have to stop to see Gwen on their way to Nancy's. I don't think I like Gwen. There has been something funny about Gwen's actions right from the start. Gwen gave Nancy that shocking pink hat. She horns into everything. She drags you in on the case, then she eases you out. I don't like Rufus either. I don't think he's a nice guy. He doesn't care who is called a murderer so long as he doesn't get involved. He and his family. I don't like his face. I don't like Helen, she hasn't got any real heart in her or she would step right up and tell people about being with Leland last night. Unless..."

Patrick brought the hot plates with the bacon and eggs and set them on the table. We sat down. I opened my mouth to go on talking. He said, "Let's let it rest while we eat. Think about something else, for a change. Shall we?"

"All right."

A few minutes passed. We spoke of this and that and then I remembered Rosalie Wong. "Isn't she a lovely-looking girl?" I said.

"All Mary's girls are pretty," Patrick said. "Mary is such a little yellow dried-up woman it doesn't seem possible that she could have so many beautiful daughters. There's a lot of mothers like Mary Wong in Chinatown. Chinese women of her generation had no chance, but now they think things will be different. They work their fingers to the bone to educate their children for the future they hope they will have back in China."

I knew he was talking about the Chinese to keep me from harping on the murder. I let my mind wander. And suddenly I heard a slight click. There was a responding click in my mind, for I remembered what it was I had forgotten—the thing that had been haunting me. I had neglected to close the hall door tightly when I followed Patrick into the apartment. Now a draught had done it for me. I relaxed.

Patrick was saying, "I used always to see Mary Wong at the Moores' and once in a while one or two of her girls would be there helping her out, but I saw them all together only once and then by accident. I was doing a job which took me into Chinatown. I went into a tenement, one of the typical apartment houses, if they can be called such, which house the local Chinese. Each family lived in one room, or at best two rooms. All families used a communal kitchen and toilet, one of each to each floor. I couldn't find the man I was looking for so I knocked on a door on the top floor to make inquiry. I chose the door at random. Mary Wong opened the door. This was her home and she and all her girls were home for the night.

"They all lived in one room. It was spotless. The beds were bunks which let down from the walls, like those in a stateroom. For a table there was a rattan tray on legs which held a teapot and a few dishes. Chests around the room served to hold clothing, and also as chairs. There was a small outside balcony and since it was a warm night the doors stood open and I could see many pots of flowering plants. The girls were spotlessly clean and well dressed. How, in a little place like that, they could do it, beats me. They welcomed me and gave me flowery tea as though I were an invited and honored guest. They hadn't even a kitchen, only a small electric plate."

I gave Patrick a straight look over my coffee cup.

"And you are a remarkable evader, Patrick Abbott. You know darn well you are trying to avoid any more talking whatever about the Leland case."

He grinned.

"You're a better dick than I am, Jeanie, darling. You're even a mind-reader."

The telephone rang.

Patrick reached for it. I could hear from across the table.

"Pat?" a voice said. "This is Gwen. I hope I haven't waked you. I just had a talk with Nancy. She tells me you've taken her case. I just wanted to tell you I'm glad."

She spoke so clearly that I heard every word. Her voice was crisp and chic.

"I'm no superman, Gwen. Don't expect any miracles."

"Is there any way I can help?"

Patrick replied with a question. "How long have you known Helen Moore, Gwen?"

There was a perceptible pause.

"Oh, ever since she and Rufus got married. Why?"

"Did you know her before that?"

Again a pause. "Why should I?"

"You get around, Gwendolyn," Patrick said.

"Is that a crack, darling?"

"Routine question, Gwen. Tell me this then—why did Leland go to Mexico?"

"Why not? He's always going to Mexico. He's got a lot of money invested down in Mexico."

"Just when did he get back to the States?"

"How should I know? He usually keeps in constant touch with our office, but it is not at all necessary that he should."

"Gwen, why didn't Phil Hannegan like Ernest Leland?"

There was another pause.

Gwen said coolly, "I don't know that he didn't."

"You know damn well he didn't like Leland, Gwen. Why don't you speak up? If you're going to play the pixie maybe I ought to start investigating you."

There was a silence.

"I told you who killed Ernest," said Gwen.

"I know you told me the Leland boy killed his father. But I've got to have more than that to go on before . . ."

Gwen cut in with a small dry laugh.

"I've told you all I can, Pat. Keep 'em flying, darling. So long."

"So long, Gwen."

Patrick's face looked pretty solemn as he replaced that receiver. He pushed his cup toward me and I refilled it and he pulled it back and put cream and sugar in without at any time being conscious of me at all. An entire change of mood seemed to have come over him from Gwen Telfer's call. He's got a hunch, I thought. He knows something suddenly. Maybe it's about Gwen. Maybe she did it herself. Why is Gwen so cagey about that Mexican trip of Leland's? Philip Hannegan went down to Mexico with Leland, I remembered. He came back first. Why?

There was a slight shuffling noise in the hall.

The light from the kitchen fanned into the hall, which was itself in darkness. Something glinted in that darkness. It was a gun. It pointed at us. The little black hole in the barrel seemed to get larger and larger while I stared.

EIGHT

In the shocked stark silence you could even hear the creepy whispery noise the rain-heavy fog made against the windows. The kitchen clock ticked. The moaning of the dreary foghorn on Alcatraz Island sounded so clearly all at once that it might have been just outside our door.

Out of the shadows a voice said, "Put your hands up!"

I glanced away from the gun to see what Patrick would do.

He put up his hands.

I did the same and my eyes slithered back to the gun.

All at once the gun wavered, looped forward, then pitched down on the uncarpeted floor of the hall with a harsh plop.

The gun-man sat down.

He sat as though poured. He slumped fluidly into a sitting posture. Then he folded with a liquid grace over on one side. His arms swam out, and his legs, and finally he lay gently sprawled, with his freckled snub-nosed face showing in profile. His eyes were closed. His wrists jutting out of the sleeves of his old soiled raincoat had a vulnerable look which, when I began to have any feeling again, got straight at my heart. His tweed jacket, gray flannel pants and plaid flannel shirt were smudged with grime and damp from the fog.

Patrick was beside him while my arms were still frozen in the air. He pocketed the gun. He felt the boy's pulse. He went through his pockets. I came alive and got my arms down and told him about leaving the door open. He walked over and turned on the ceiling lights in the hall and went to see if the front door was now closed and locked. He returned and in the bright light he examined the gun. There wasn't even one cartridge in the .32-calibre Colt automatic. The entire clip was absent and there was no cartridge in the chamber.

"No wonder he fainted when he pulled this gun," Patrick said, dropping it into his own pocket.

"Oh." I came closer. Patrick was checking over the contents of a wallet. "Want me to get cold water and things, Pat?"

"Just let him alone."

The boy lay motionless. His thick dark lashes made curved shadows on his young freckled cheeks.

They flickered. His eyelids lifted from wide gray eyes.

"What—goes—on?" he asked, without moving.

"A fine housebreaker you turned out to be," Patrick said.

The boy's mouth twitched. He closed his eyes and lay without moving again, as if gathering his strength.

Patrick said, "Do you often go gunning without bullets, Chris?"

"Somebody snitched them, somewhere." He hitched himself slowly up on one elbow. "How come you know my name?"

"I frisked you while you were blacked out," Patrick said. With a flick of a smile he said, "You Connecticut Yanks have funny notions about the Wild West. We use doorbells out here, same as you, Chris."

Chris looked embarrassed.

"I'm sorry. You see, I slipped into the building when that elevator man wasn't looking, and managed to get upstairs, and I had just got to your door when I heard the cage coming down from up above so—well, your door was open so I walked in. I heard you talking about me on the phone. I got suspicious. This isn't a trap, is it?"

"What do you mean trap?"

"You won't turn me over to the police?"

"Should I, Chris?"

The boy sat up.

"I didn't kill my father, as you said over the phone."

"I don't remember that I said that exactly. Like a cigarette?"

"I don't smoke."

"How about a drink?"

"It wouldn't stay down if I had it, Mr. Abbott."

Patrick's eyes smiled.

"How come you know *my* name?"

Chris grinned pallidly. "I came up here specially to see you," he said. "I won't tell you who sent me, but I guess you must know I'm in a fix."

Chris looked as if he was about to faint again and I thought it was time for me to interfere.

"He's hungry," I said. He didn't deny it, and I said, "I'll fix you some bacon and eggs and some coffee, Chris."

"Could I have milk?" Chris asked. "Milk sends me. It's social suicide to say so, though."

"Sure you can have milk," Patrick said. He stood up and gave the boy a hand up. "There's a bath along the hall on your right. By the time you wash up supper will be ready."

Chris halted a short way along the hall.

"You're not going to hand me over to the police?"

"That seems to be on your mind, Chris."

"Well, I sort of broke into this apartment."

"We'll talk that over while you eat," Patrick said.

"I don't want to put you to any trouble, though . . ."

"Scram along and get washed!" Patrick said.

"The poor kid," I said, as we were fixing his supper. "What made him faint like that, dear?"

"Maybe he scared himself into it. Maybe it's short rations."

"Bacon and eggs send me," Chris said, after he had consumed all we had in the icebox. "So do toast and strawberry jam. Breakfast is my favorite meal."

"How long since you've had a square meal?" Patrick asked.

"Not very long," Chris said. We knew he was lying. "I guess I sort of forgot to eat . . ."

"There was just thirty-nine cents in your pockets, Chris."

The boy reddened. "It took me longer to get out to California than I thought. This country is so darned big, Mr. Abbott. And I hadn't brought enough money along to start with. Of course I expected to go right to work, if I couldn't get into the army. Only . . ."

"Only what?"

"I'd got to see my father and settle with him first."

"You came out here to kill him," Patrick said.

Chris dropped his gaze. "I don't deny it. And maybe I changed my mind about that by the time I got here, but just the same I meant to give him a good hard scare. He deserved that, at least."

Patrick said, "I noticed you haven't got a license to carry that gun?"

"It's not my gun," Chris said. "But I don't want anybody to get into trouble because of that." He wrinkled his forehead. "Say, how did you know that?"

"I told you I went through your pockets. When people come into other people's houses and pull guns they deserve to be searched. Guns make people who carry them a lot of trouble. I never have one on me myself. Even an unloaded gun can often get you into a nasty fix."

"That part's funny, too," Chris said. "That gun was loaded when I got to San Francisco. Somewhere or other somebody snitched my ammunition. The clip and everything in it."

"When do you think that happened?"

"I don't know."

We were sitting around the kitchen table. Patrick started making a cigarette. "Suppose you tell me the whole story?"

"Will you help me? If I do?"

"I will if I can and if I think you deserve it."

Chris took a moment to consider what he had to tell. "Well, there isn't much to say really. My father and mother were separated before I was old enough to know what was going on. My mother went back to live with my aunt in the house in Hartford, Connecticut, which has been in our family a hundred and fifty years. The house belongs to my aunt. My mother took what she inherited in cash and my father used it up to get his start. He grew up in Hartford, too. The family didn't like him. My mother ran away and married him and they came out here. I was born here. When we went back East my aunt took us in and my mother and my aunt both taught school to make a living, and when I was eight years old my father started sending me away to school."

I remembered that in the East a great many boys were sent to exclusive boarding schools. It is considered much more the thing to do there than it is in the West.

"It cost him plenty, but of course I didn't know it. I had everything, but never much cash. He worked it so that I had credit everywhere, even at hotels in New York. I could step around high, wide and handsome when I was only fifteen or sixteen, though I hardly ever had as much as ten dollars all at once in my pocket."

"How old are you now?" I inquired.

Patrick answered. "Seventeen," he said, and when Chris stared at him, he added, smiling, "I read your draft card, Chris."

Chris said, "I was quite some guy. Maybe I'd take a bunch of boys from school down to New York for a week end and run up bills for maybe as high as five hundred dollars and my old man would fork it out without so much as a squawk. I thought he was made of money. And meantime my own mother was dying of t.b., and she didn't even have the price of the ordinary good care. And I didn't even know it. But he knew it! That was why I could do what I pleased and the sky was the limit. That was how he punished my mother for walking out on him long ago. Here he was, rolling in dough, and there she was, dying because she hadn't proper care, and there I was so damn dumb I didn't know what was going on."

"Why did he do that?" Patrick asked.

"He was getting even with her for leaving him, Mr. Abbott."

"You are sure, Chris?"

Chris nodded his head. "My aunt told me the whole story last summer. It was when I was starting to college. I wanted to study medicine and my father said I had to study law. It was the first time I'd come up against anything like that. I never did see him, you know. Everything was done through lawyers. I talked about school to my aunt. I wanted to start pre-medic. You see, I wasn't home much, ever, after I started away to school. My father saw to that. I would get a week or so at home three or four times a year, and then I would be sent away on trips, or to camp, or back to school. I didn't think much about that till my aunt told me last summer that it was my father's way of keeping me away from my mother. I didn't realize that the schools he was sending me to were beyond my mother's means and that she thought the thing to do was to let me go ahead and do nothing herself to interfere, since any kind of argument might stop him doing anything for me at all. There wasn't any sort of agreement about me, you see."

"Was there a divorce?"

"Yes. My mother got one shortly after she went back East. She didn't ask for anything. It wasn't contested in any way. My aunt said that if she asked for a settlement he would have found a way to keep her from getting anything. I don't know. I do know though that he used all her money to get his start and that he deliberately let her die when he could have helped her . . ."

"You're positive about that?"

"Positive. My aunt kept copies of letters she wrote him about four years ago begging him for help. He didn't even answer. After my mother had to stay in bed, my aunt did all she could on her salary. She couldn't afford a nurse all the time even. And here I was, as dumb bunny-dumb as they come . . ."

"When did you say your aunt told you all this?"

"Last summer. When I didn't want to study law and my father told me I had to. She got mad and told me everything, then."

"And why did you wait all these months to—take action?"

"I don't know. I guess it took a while to sink in. Then at school nothing went right. I hated my courses and—well, all at once, something came over me, everything seemed to get straight. It seemed to me that my father had murdered my mother and that all he deserved was the same thing. I got the idea all at once. I decided I had to do it. I borrowed my roommate's gun. . . ."

Chris must be very susceptible to suggestion, I was thinking, as Patrick said, "Your roommate had a gun?"

"He comes from a shooting family," Chris said. "They all have guns. This gun really is his father's. I'd learned to shoot, so . . ."

He hesitated.

"Okay. Go on." Patrick had glanced at the clock. It was almost eleven-thirty.

"Well, that's all. We rustled up forty dollars between us and I took the gun and hitched my way out. I arrived here with only five bucks. I was careful on the way, but it took me nine days to get here. Then that hotel Mr. Hannegan led me around to set me back four bucks for one night, and so . . ."

"That was night before last?"

"Check."

"Where did you sleep last night?"

Chris grinned.

"I got a bed in a flophouse for a quarter. I had to cut down on my overhead, see."

"And you've eaten on forty-six cents for two days . . ."

"Well, something like that. Skip it, Mr. Abbott. I can work and I'm going to, but I'd got the idea I had to see the old man and tell him off first. I'd got over wanting to shoot him. I guess I haven't got any guts. I intended going back to that same place to try to get a bunk tonight when I saw in a newspaper that he had been murdered. I bought it and read that the police were looking for me. The paper said that I had boasted to that Miss Telfer who was associated in some way in business with my father that I had come out here specifically to kill him. I got scared. I didn't know what to do. I decided to come to ask you what to do. But I haven't got any money, or anything . . ."

"Who told you to come to me?"

Chris hesitated, then said, "Would you mind if I didn't tell you that, Mr. Abbott?"

"Suit yourself," Patrick said. "Now I want to ask a few questions. First, did you follow us from Nancy Leland's house tonight?"

A glazed look crossed the freckled face.

"No. No, I didn't."

"Do you know Nancy Leland?"

"No-o."

"What will you do now?"

"I—well, I don't think I'd better go back to that same place I went to last night—it was pretty awful anyway . . ."

"We can offer you a bedroom and a bath," I said. I was speaking out of turn, but there was that maid's room separated from this kitchen by its own little hall, and here he was, that nice tired boy, talking about going back to some flophouse.

"Thanks, Mrs. Abbott, but . . ."

"You aren't thinking of turning it down?" Patrick demanded.

"Well—whatever you think . . ."

The boy's face had brightened. Suddenly it went clouded.

"I haven't any money," he said. "You have to charge fees for what you do, don't you?"

"Forget it," Patrick said. The boy looked as if he was about to break down and cry. I jumped up and went off to bring him towels and a suit of Patrick's pajamas. The bed itself was made up. I felt like crying, too. I wondered why that boy got at you so. Patrick went off to show him his room and I stacked the dishes. My mind hovered like a mother over that boy. He had eaten every darn thing I planned to use for breakfast but it didn't matter now at all.

NINE

The night-fog now lay over the hill thick, wet and icily cold. As we walked the streetlamps showed up one at a time and looked like blurs of cold fire. A tree-branch or a portion of a shrub would appear as if by stealth, and then stealthily vanish.

We even felt like wrongdoers, or I did rather, because we were calling on Philip Hannegan without warning him first, and also because we had skulked out of the apartment house, to avoid Vincent Smith. We had walked down. We had waited till he was aloft in the elevator to slip out through the lobby. He was too suspicious. It was best not to make him curious in any way.

We had postponed going to talk to that waiter in the Mexican place because seeing Philip Hannegan was definitely more urgent.

We passed by Nancy Leland's house without even seeing it because of the fog, and turned left up a short incline into a dead-end street. Philip Hannegan's small one-story house sat at the very crest of Russian Hill. It was invisible, but as we walked along the flagged path from the gate two spots of luminescence which were lanterns singled out his door.

I tried to change Patrick's mind. "He's expecting someone." Patrick walked straight on. I said, trotting beside him, "Couldn't we go away and come back? And phone first, the way I wanted to do in the first place?"

"This way is best."

"It's very bad manners," I said.

A portion of the house materialized. The pale wide blotch on the left of the door was from the living-room lights shining through closed Venetian blinds.

Patrick put a finger on the bell-button.

Philip opened the door promptly. Then he stood in the way of our entering, looking anything but hospitable. He was dressed just as he'd been when we met him at dinner with Gwen Telfer.

He said, "Why—hello."

"May we come in?" Patrick asked. Philip didn't budge. "You're getting the house full of fog," Patrick remarked amiably, as clouds of the stuff went puffing in. Philip stepped back slightly. Patrick eased us in. We stood in a small entrance hall with a mirror, one chair, a container for umbrellas and hooks for coats.

Philip closed the door all but a crack, through which the fog continued to seep. He stood with one hand on the knob.

"I'm sorry. I'm expecting a—visitor."

Divesting himself of his raincoat, and then helping me out of mine, while I boiled inside with shame for our behavior, Patrick replied blithely, "We won't take long, Phil."

He did not stir.

"If you had rung me up . . ."

"We stood a chance of being overheard. We've got a guest. Thanks for sending us Chris, Phil."

Philip grinned wryly and, his hand still on the slightly open door, said, "So he told you I sent him?"

"Nope. But it had to be you or Nancy and I felt pretty sure it wasn't Nancy."

Philip closed the door.

"The kid called me up. He seemed pretty desperate. I can't believe he had anything to do with his father's murder."

Patrick said, "The police may not trouble the boy, unless they think arresting him would be one way of working on Nancy. They really do think Nancy killed Leland."

Philip said, "What rot!" Then he said, "You'd better come on in."

He pushed open a door which led into a hall. A few steps along he opened the door into the living room.

It was a big room, longer than wide, paneled in dark wood, with a lot of solid-looking furniture, many books, sensibly shaded lamps, and many windows behind the closed blinds. A wood fire in the big fireplace had been lately refueled. The glasses and the chromium of the bar in one corner gleamed in the firelight and lamplight.

The room smelled like tobacco and pinewood.

Philip owned this house. He had sublet it furnished during those three years of active service.

In this dark-toned room his blondness was striking.

We sat down on the sofa. Philip took his stand by the mantel. We had got in, I was thinking, with acute discomfort, but Phil meant to make the interview brief.

"I sent the kid to you, Pat, and also I tried to reach you to say he might be there," he said. "He phoned me for advice. That was a couple of hours or so ago. I didn't care if you knew I'd sent him. I told him not to tell it around mostly to keep Gwen Telfer out of my hair. Gwen has made up her mind that Chris did it, and you know Gwen. I don't care for myself, but I think the less notice Gwen calls to the kid the better it will be for everybody."

"Gwen might be right," Patrick said.

"Maybe. But I had a long talk with Chris in my office the other afternoon when he came in to ask where his father was. There's no real harm in him, in my opinion. He's impulsive. He idealized his mother. He got in a state of mind and he got hold of that automatic and so on, but believe me, by the time he got here all the will to kill had gone out of him. Or so I think."

"You saw his gun?"

"I told you that I took it from him and put it in a drawer in my desk."

"And it was gone when you got back to the office this morning?"

"I told you that."

"Did you remove the cartridges from the gun?"

Philip frowned. "It didn't occur to me. I didn't think he would take it back, you see. What's this all about? Leland wasn't shot, was he?"

"I'm curious about what happened to his ammunition, and why it would be stolen."

Philip asked suddenly, "Pat, who killed Leland?"

Patrick said, "Leland was killed by somebody who knew how to kill. It was a carefully deliberated murder planned by somebody who knew him well, somebody who knew his habits and got ready for it in advance. And whoever did it took no chances that Leland might stay alive. Or, I might say, that his dying might be noisy. A gun was not employed."

Philip Hannegan turned his gaze onto the fire.

Patrick said, "It doesn't look like a kid's job, unless the kid is a sort of pervert. I would agree with you, on short acquaintance, that Chris is impulsive. He doesn't seem—this is a snap judgment, and I admit it— capable of planning what happened to his father. Whoever murdered Leland knew this city fairly well, I think, and thought out in advance what a good idea it would be to send the body in a runaway car down that particular hill so that it would likely be badly mangled and throw the police off the track. Immediately after death there would as a rule in such an accident have been considerable bleeding. There wasn't any, because the body, perfectly relaxed, had slipped down in the front of the seat, and had escaped being cut by any flying glass. The odor of cyanide might have been present had there been any bleeding, but with the fumes of gasoline about the murderer might count on that's passing unnoticed."

Philip Hannegan stood with one hand thrust in his coat pocket, looking into the fire.

At the slightest sound outside the house he would lift his head quickly and listen. I wondered who was coming. He seemed pretty intense.

Patrick said, "I am saying all this because I imagine it was what the murderer had in mind when planning this murder."

Philip drummed on the mantel with his fingertips. He said nothing.

Patrick said, "Maybe Rufus Moore killed Leland."

Philip Hannegan was so astonished at this statement that he could not for the moment make any reply. He stood and gaped.

Then he said, "You're barking up the wrong tree there, Pat. Rufus was in Los Angeles."

"You can kill by deputy," said Patrick.

"What do you mean?"

"Rufus's wife was in San Francisco when Leland was murdered."

Philip Hannegan's jaw dropped. There was a flat sort of silence. The fire sputtered. A piece of a log fell down and sent up a flock of sparks.

He shook his blond head. "You're wrong, Pat. She went to San Diego that night. I saw her at the airport when I caught the six-thirty plane for San Francisco, the plane that Leland was supposed to connect with."

"She came to San Francisco, Phil. With Leland."

For a moment Philip Hannegan said nothing. He kept drumming on the mantel with his fingertips. "Well, I don't want to get mixed up in that angle, if you don't mind. I do know that her mother is ill. If not, they've been keeping up that fiction for a long time. Elaine was devoted to her mother. Helen was, I mean."

"You didn't kill Leland, did you, Phil?"

"My—God—Almighty!" Philip Hannegan said.

Patrick's eyes were narrowed. "Routine question. Mild, compared to what the police may hand you when your time comes. It's plain as your face that you're in love with Nancy Leland. Incidentally, I saw you duck behind a bush when we came out of her house tonight, Phil. What made you go there?"

Philip shrugged. "I didn't go in."

"The house is under police surveillance."

Philip was restless. His hands worked and he seemed at a loss what to say.

"I wanted to be sure that Nancy would take counsel. I was afraid to phone. I thought I might go there under cover of the fog. I'm worried, Pat. For her. I went to try to talk to her. Then I realized I was being a dope and didn't go in. You're the one to talk her into being careful, Pat."

"Maybe. Tell me, why is Gwen Telfer so anxious to protect Nancy?"

Philip shrugged. "I think what Gwen is doing is calling more attention to Nancy than anything else. But I don't think Gwen realizes that. She's tricky in business, but I really wouldn't call her subtle."

Patrick said abruptly, "You hated Leland's guts. Why?"

Philip did not answer.

"Did you hate him enough to murder him, Phil?"

"Probably," Philip said drily. "But somebody beat me to it."

"Did you hate him because of Nancy?"

"Not consciously."

"Then why?"

Philip's fingers closed like a vise over the edge of the mantel. He was silent. The room seemed to take on his silence. The fire sputtered in a sullen fashion.

"He was avaricious," Philip said finally. "If he wanted something he took it. He didn't care what depths of human suffering followed on any act of his, so long as he got what he wanted. Yet I don't think many realized this. I guess I could not prove it even to protect Nancy. I could try. I can tell you a few things, when the time comes, if it will be of any help to her."

"Better tell them now, Phil."

Philip shook his head.

Patrick let it ride. "Rufus wanted that marriage to last. He could have stopped it in the first place if he hadn't. Nancy always tried to do whatever Rufus wished."

Philip said disgustedly, "Rufus is dead from the neck up."

"Rufus didn't want the divorce," Patrick said. "He was afraid it would cost him his job."

"Darn right it would," Philip said.

"Then Leland was vindictive?"

"That's drawing it mild," Philip said.

Patrick took another tack.

"Gwen says she knows the contents of Leland's last will. Maybe Rufus knew then, too. Nancy is fond of Rufus, still very susceptible to his wishes, as we said. Rufus might have murdered Leland to keep the money in the family, so he would have it to do with as he pleased."

"We're repeating ourselves," Philip replied. "As I said, Rufus was in Los Angeles that night."

"And, as I said, you can kill by deputy. His wife was here. We saw her and Leland in a nightclub together."

Philip moved his shoulders.

"Well, could be. But I still don't think either Rufus or Helen would take such a chance."

"She tells lies," I put in. "She told Nancy she went to San Diego, same as she told you. You can't be two places at once. Even I can deduce that item, Phil."

Philip said, "Helen's a fairly common type, Jean. She tried to get into pictures. She called herself Elaine something. She didn't make the grade, because—I'm told—she's a common type, looks too much like lots of other girls. So, maybe you saw somebody else."

"Nope," I said. "We saw Helen. She was wearing the same furs, the same diamond, the same hat. We didn't see somebody else, Phil."

Philip gave in suddenly, and talked.

"Well, anyway—well, here goes, if it will be any help to Nancy, which I doubt. I was down in L.A. yesterday, as you know. I was in Rufus's office just before leaving for the airport. Helen rang him up. He told her he would have to work late and suggested that she go to a show and meet him at nine o'clock for dinner. They arranged the place. It was Helen, all right. He's nuts about her and it always shows in his face when he's talking to her or about her. Nothing was said about a sick mother. When by sheer chance I ran into Helen at the airport half an hour or so later she told me she was going to San Diego because her mother had taken a sudden turn for the worse. Well, things like that happen suddenly. There was no reason why she couldn't've got the word after she talked to Rufus. I feel like a heel telling you this, by the way."

"Did she go to the airport to meet Leland?"

"He was not mentioned."

"You called her Elaine. Have you known her long?"

"She's been married to Rufus about two years, I think."

Patrick let the evasion pass. He asked abruptly, "Was she Leland's mistress?"

"My God! How would I know?" Philip barked.

"News gets around."

"Well, I never heard it, if she ever was," Philip said. "I'd say offhand she wasn't, but I don't know anything about it, for a fact."

"You went down to Mexico with Leland?" Patrick asked.

There was a slight change in Philip's demeanor. He said nothing.

"What happened down there?" Patrick asked. "Every time it has come up . . ."

Philip cut in, "Look here, this is strictly between ourselves, Pat, and it is probably cockeyed and will probably have no bearing on Leland's murder or anything else, but Leland insisted on my going with him to Mexico and down there he tried to get *me* murdered. Now, don't laugh, please."

"I'm not," Patrick said grimly.

Philip, having got started, talked rapidly on, in a low urgent voice.

"His excuse for taking me along with him was that he wanted to invest in a luxury hotel being planned for a town on Lake Chappala, and he wanted me there to talk over future advertising ideas. No one would do for some reason except me. Once there he kept me busy driving around looking at the scenery and such. One afternoon I was sent without him. The driver stopped us on the edge of a cliff with a view over a deep valley. He got out of the car. A minute later a light truck came tearing round the blind turn back of us and bumped into our car and knocked it over the precipice. I escaped by luck. I happened to grab onto a bush growing out of the very edge of the rock as I was thrown out." Philip's eyes were angry. "Okay. The next afternoon I was nearly run down in a narrow street in the town. The driver was the same man who had previously driven the truck. And I saw his face that time when he came after me. He meant to get me. Leland had gone on to Mexico City that morning. I came back here without joining him. I meant to have it out with him the first chance I got—but, of course, he was bumped off before I got that chance." Philip said grimly, "I feel as if I'd done it myself somehow, by remote control."

Patrick asked, "Would he want you out of the way because of Nancy?"

Philip took a moment to answer. "It's something else, Pat. I don't know what, exactly. I think he thinks I knew something I have no knowledge of knowing, if that makes sense."

"Was there really to be a hotel? Or was that only an excuse to get you down where it was handier to bump you off?"

"There will be a hotel, even without Leland. No—I have the feeling that he thinks I discovered something. Down there. Something he didn't want known. I speak Spanish and he didn't and—but what it was all about God only knows."

The doorbell rang. A mere tinkle.

Alert on the instant Philip said, "Stay where you are. I'll only be a minute."

He crossed to the door, opened it, stepped into the hall, closed the door, opened the door into the entry, and closed it before he opened the front door.

Already Patrick had got up and was crossing the room swiftly to the hall door. He opened it and stood listening.

From the sofa I could hear nothing. I sat in an agony of anguish because I was afraid Philip would catch Patrick listening. I heard no greeting at the front door and no good-bye. I did hear the door close. On that very instant, Patrick had closed the hall door and when Phil returned was back on the sofa, his long legs crossed, his appearance as nonchalant as when Philip had left us.

Philip crossed directly to the portable bar, saying, "Now we can settle down and talk. We'll have a drink and then I'll try to answer your questions."

Patrick had risen. "Sorry, Phil. We've got to beat it."

"But now everything's all set?" Philip objected.

"We'll have to continue this tomorrow, Phil. We mustn't leave that kid alone too long. How about coming for breakfast?"

"Yes, do," I said, wondering, however, if there would be anything to eat.

Patrick would have no dallying over the leavetaking. We walked straight out and got on our things. The little entrance hall was smoky with fog. It smelled of a sense-stirring perfume. It was Helen Moore's perfume. I had encountered it twice before.

TEN

The fog was fast turning into mist. Down by the water the foghorn moaned. Things which loomed so abruptly in their queer trailing draperies were so wraithlike that I shivered at the sound of our own padding footsteps as we went back down the incline into Jones Street. I listened all the time for the light wily steps of a follower, knowing while I listened that I was being foolish, and that, that last time, the pursuant footfalls might even have been those of some casual passer-by, who had taken flight out of momentary panic when we ourselves stopped short and gave chase.

What was Patrick thinking about? He kept very silent. Had he divined something in what Philip Hannegan had told him which had escaped me? Maybe Philip had really killed Leland. He had good cause. He had a sharp, impetuous will. He could, I fancied, hate with a splendid vigor. He would be inclined, or so I imagined, to retaliate swiftly. The war had made certain men lawless. Perhaps Philip was such a one.

All Leland cared about was getting what he wanted, Philip had said. No matter the cost in human degradation, he'd said.

Philip did not care much for Helen Moore, I decided. Elaine, he had referred to her. I decided that he had known her longer and more intimately than he had said. He had evaded that question.

Yet, when you considered his blond wholesome face it was impossible to associate him in any way with dark intrigue. He was so clean-looking, so fair-haired, so wholesomely attractive. He had a shining look always.

Well, if he was a good hater he might be a good lover, too, and therefore just the man for obstinate, attractive Nancy Leland.

We passed Nancy's house, a dim and somehow fluent shape in the fog-mist. It stood in darkness. Nancy was there, and Rufus, and in the garage apartment were the two Wongs. Helen—had Helen Moore returned to that dark house? She had come out—to see Philip Hannegan.

Why? What did he know that she so wanted suppressed that she had gone out to see Philip in this damp, dripping weather? The fog would be hard on her hair. It would make trouble for her make-up, her minks if she had worn them, for the dozen artificialities with which she turned herself out. She would not have gone to see Philip without some urgent cause.

I glanced up at Patrick. His raincoat collar was turned up. His hat brim was turned down. He looked taciturn and grim—what I could see of him. It was no time to ask questions. Sounds carry too well in heavy weather. He probably wouldn't answer them, if asked.

We walked on, down the slow incline, turning right into Green Street.

All at once Patrick stopped me.

There they were again! Behind us light, nervous footsteps sounded briefly, then stopped.

We stood listening.

That was all. There was nothing else. It might indeed have been an echo from the hill beside us. This was where we had heard it before. It was the same. It had a crazy pattern, the senselessness and unreality of an echo.

We walked on. I felt icy with fear. I clung tight to Patrick's arm. Twice he stopped us. But we heard nothing more. We got to the apartment house and climbed the steps. There was no one in the lobby. The cage was down, but Vincent Smith was not in sight. We climbed the five floors to our apartment, trotting up the last one, in spite of my lack of breath, because we could hear our own telephone ringing monotonously. Patrick unlocked the door. The hall light was on as we had left it and, after making certain that the door was closed this time, I followed Patrick toward the kitchen where he went to take the call. He turned on the lights. He dived for the phone.

"Excuse it, please," the operator said.

Patrick cradled the receiver. He took out the makings of a cigarette. He stood in his raincoat, shaking the yellow tobacco onto the tissue. I faced him across the room.

"Is somebody always following us, Pat?" He rolled the cigarette and licked it and made no reply. "If so, who is it?"

He smiled a crooked smile.

"Somebody who wants to know what we're up to, probably."

"Don't make jokes," I said. "Even I would know that. Look, do you realize that it was Helen Moore who came to Phil Hannegan's tonight?"

"I recognized her voice when I listened at the hall door," he said.

"Oh. I could smell her perfume, as we came out. Why did she come there, do you think?"

"My guess is that Phil knows something she wants kept dark," Patrick said.

"It's about Leland," I said. I felt excited. "He must have told her something, in the plane. Or maybe—maybe she killed him and she knows, or thinks, Phil may know . . ."

Patrick lit his cigarette and offered to make me one, which I declined. He said, "It may be something else entirely. That Elaine of his was pretty automatic. Maybe she thinks he knows something she'd rather Rufus didn't find out."

"Oh, he wouldn't tell that sort of thing. Not Phil."

"You're right."

I asked, again, "Is somebody following us everywhere, dear? Or do I imagine it?"

Patrick frowned. "You don't imagine it, Jean. I kept hearing our follower all the way from Phil's. Whoever it is takes a shorter step than either of ours and while it is almost noiseless the difference in the rhythm makes it perceptible."

"You've got wonderful ears, darling. You can hear the grass grow. Well, what are we going to feed Phil for breakfast?"

The telephone rang. Patrick answered, and I eased over to listen.

"That you, Pat? Where have you been?"

"Out walking. Such a lovely night, Sam."

"Yeah, isn't it? You didn't go back to Nancy Leland's?"

"What do you think?"

The voice sounded conciliatory. "Now, see here, Pat. You're no fool, whatever else you are. I'll tell you why I'm calling. It's about that Leland boy. Leland had a son, a kid about seventeen. We had him checked on in New Haven, Connecticut, and found out he's not a bad kid, though inclined to be hasty. He's out here, we knew that already from—well, the source is confidential . . ."

"Miss Telfer gets around, Sam."

"Oh. Well, what of it? The thing is, your night man there, Vincent Smith, saw the kid hanging around tonight, and after that he disappeared. He is said to have a gun. I'm calling you to warn you to be on the lookout for him, and to take it easy."

"Thanks, Sam. I'll do that. Where are you, by the way?"

"Down near Howard and Sixth. I told you we were working on a big case, got a set-back when one of the gang who was going to turn state's evidence got killed. Well, I'm off to get a little shut-eye, I hope."

"It's very kind of you to keep tipping me off, Sam. What makes you think the Leland boy would come here?"

I could hear Bradish's laugh. "Maybe he wants a detective. There ought to be good money in a client like that. Make it easier to lose Nancy Leland."

"Right," Patrick said.

I was distracted by a slight movement, somewhere. There was, however, no sound. I wondered if Chris was moving about in his little room across the hall. If both doors were closed he ought not to be disturbed, though. I glanced all around. My glance took in the door leading to the service stairs to the right of the white-enameled sink.

"I want to have a talk with you, Pat," Bradish said.

"Come up for breakfast, Sam," Patrick said.

Shocked at the prospect of having to feed Bradish along with Phil Hannegan, and Chris again, and with nothing whatever to feed them, I whirled on Patrick.

I didn't say anything. With a slight gesture he warned me to keep still.

His eyes were fixed on the door. The receiver was at his ear. He was listening to Bradish, but he was watching that door. He reached out suddenly with his other arm and pulled me behind him, so that my body was shielded from that direction by his own.

"Well, so long, Pat," Bradish said finally.

"So long, Sam."

Patrick cradled the receiver and with the agility of a cat crossed the room and yanked open the door. It was not locked, though we had left it locked.

Helen Moore almost fell into the room.

She recovered her balance and her poise at once. Even though she must have known she was minus her glamour.

Clever woman, I thought. Her tinted hair was stringy from the fog. Most of her make-up was missing. So were her minks. She wore what was probably Rufus's tweed top-coat over the gray flannel dress she had been wearing when she arrived at Nancy's last evening.

She stood with her hands linked, her smile rueful.

"That's what I get for slipping in the back way," she said.

"It's rather a stiff climb," Patrick said. He gestured at the dinette. "Will you sit down? Have a cup of coffee, or a drink?"

"Nothing, thanks. I mustn't take the time. I don't want Rufus to miss me. You went to see Philip tonight, didn't you?"

She had moved under the center light and her appearance was further ravaged by its glare.

Yet she looked sincere, earnest, and her rather flat voice, heightened by emotion, had a better quality than I had given it credit.

We kept standing, grouped around the utility table in the middle of the kitchen.

"I knew that in a place this size there would be a night porter or someone. I didn't want to be seen. I used to have friends who lived here. I remembered that the garage for the house is under the building, with a back entrance. I slipped in, and made my way up the service stairs. It took a little time, and I was almost caught once or twice."

"You came here directly from Hannegan's?"

She said, "He told you I came there?"

"No. Jean recognized your perfume in the hall."

Helen smiled. "And I saw your things. Phil was careful not to say who was there, but I saw the things you're wearing now. I was pretty sure they were yours."

Our raincoats. Damp from the weather. We still had them on.

"Would you like to sit in the living room?" I asked. "It's pretty terrible, but if you don't like kitchens . . ."

"I love kitchens," Helen said, with such energy I felt sure she meant it. I began to like her a little. "I should have knocked, of course, I'm not usually so rude. But I felt certain just before I got to this floor that I was being followed. It was queer. I turned the knob—I could hear you inside . . ."

"That's all right, Mrs. Moore," Patrick said.

It wasn't, entirely, because we didn't know how it had got unlocked.

Helen asked, "Did Philip Hannegan ask you to come there tonight?"

Patrick answered. "Certainly not. Why?"

Helen bit her lip. "For a moment I distrusted him," she said. "I thought he had double-crossed me, perhaps. I thought . . ."

She broke off. Her ages-old eyes set in the sockets of a young face moved from one to the other of us.

"I'll tell you. I went deliberately to see Philip because—because I don't want anything, ever, to come between him and Nancy. It was for sentiment, and nothing else."

"Oh," I said. Impressed favorably.

"You went by arrangement?" Patrick asked.

"I phoned him," Helen said. "I planned it all out. I don't know if you know the upstairs in Nancy's house?" Patrick nodded. Helen said, "Then you know that there are two bedrooms which connect through a bath. One used to be Rufus's and the other was his father's. That house has phone connections and push-bells in all the rooms because Mr. Moore was a semi-invalid for many years and Rufus did everything to make his father's life easy and comfortable. I took one of the phones to my room. There are only two now, there used to be three or four but they gave the extras up because of war shortages. I expected a call from San Diego—or rather, there was a chance of a call, since my mother is gravely ill—

and I had that as an excuse. But I wanted also to call up Philip Hannegan. I *had* to talk to him."

We stood listening.

"But, because you saw Philip first I have come here to say to you what I wanted to say to Phil," she said. "Listen, first of all, you must believe me when I tell you that I went there tonight for the very same reason that I came to San Francisco with Ernest Leland last night—entirely for Nancy's sake."

My chest was tight with excitement. She is clever, I thought. She remembers us from last night. She knows we've got her. She wants us on her side, so she is putting her cards on the table. *All her cards?* That would be seen.

Helen rested her ox-blood fingertips on the table.

"You two saw me last night. You came into that dive Ernest took me to—because he didn't want us seen together, I think—and you kept looking at me. At least Jean did. Jean is very beautiful, it would be impossible for me not to remember her, of course. And you, too, Pat. You make me think of Gary Cooper."

Buttering us up, I thought. I didn't like her so well now.

"Did you go to talk to Phil because you saw me last night with Leland?" she asked then.

Patrick said, "We went to see Phil because of my client. Young Chris Leland. Phil sent Chris to me."

"But I thought you were working for Nancy?"

"Naturally," Patrick fibbed. "Of course."

"Oh. You can have two clients? At the same time?"

"Why not? If you are convinced that both are innocent."

"I see. Well, I've known Phil a long time. I used to see him at parties in Hollywood. He had a job then in Los Angeles. I tried to get into pictures, you know. I called myself Elaine Bishop. My mother spent a fortune backing me, but I couldn't make the grade. Now I'm married, and I've forgotten my ambitions, and I'm happy. I want to have a family and live an everyday life. I want the same for Nancy. I am very fond of Nancy and it was for her sake entirely that I came up here with Ernest last night and went out to see Philip tonight. You see, Phil saw me at the airport in Los Angeles, and I was afraid he might think that I met Ernest there deliberately"—she shuddered and said—"Ernest Leland is the last person in the world I would want an intrigue with. He was a ruthless, horrible man."

She spoke as if she meant it.

Patrick asked, "Why?"

"I can't tell you that. I'm sorry."

"If it would help any to get it off your chest . . ."

"It won't."

"But Rufus admires him?" I said.

"Rufus does not know—all I know."

"You met Leland then by appointment at the airport in Los Angeles?" Patrick asked.

"Oh, no. Quite by chance. I was going to San Diego. Ernest's plane from Albuquerque was late. That plane from the east makes connections both for San Francisco and San Diego, incidentally, but there's a wait for the San Diego plane, which I was taking, and I still had plenty of time. Right away I saw that Ernest was in a state of mind. I tried to persuade him to be patient. There are several other flights to San Francisco during the evening and he could surely have got a seat on one of them. But nothing could hold him. Then I got frightened. I made up my mind he was going to make trouble for Nancy. There was nothing in this world I could do for my mother now, but at least I could help Nancy, so when he chartered a private plane I climbed aboard. He was too upset and in too much of a hurry to prevent it."

"You seem to have known him very well?"

Helen answered bitterly, "Very well."

"Would your knowledge—whatever it is—help Nancy Leland?"

Helen hesitated, then said, "If it will—I'll tell all I know. But not now. I can't tell it to you now. I can't even tell you why."

Patrick did not press her. I knew he would take another slant at it, get at her roundabout.

He said, "Suppose you tell me what happened exactly. First, you went to the Los Angeles airport to go to San Diego. You saw Leland . . ."

"I saw Philip Hannegan first," Helen said. "That was something else to worry about. I wanted to explain to Phil tonight why I had come up here with Ernest, in case he knew that I came. I don't know why he should, but he might. I shall tell Rufus, but not now. He gets in such a dither. If he knew I was with Ernest Leland just before he was murdered he would be so worried he would make all sorts of blunders—no, he must not know it yet—no, no!"

"All right. Go on with what happened."

"Well, Ernest arrived in Los Angeles and I came here with him. His car had been sent out to the airport. He didn't have any luggage. He left it in Los Angeles to come up on a later plane. He certainly seemed in a frightful stew. He hardly seemed to know or care if I was along. Besides, it was too noisy on the plane to talk. When we got into his car he said talking bothered him when he was driving, that we would talk at dinner. He seemed then quite reasonable, and nice. When we got into the city he cut over on Kearny Street and pulled up near Portsmouth Square. He got out of the car and went into the Square. I got the impression he was meeting someone near the Stevenson memorial, but I saw him speak to no one. Of course it was night, well along toward eleven o'clock by that time. He came back and drove straight to that Mexican place where you saw us. He let me out and parked around the corner. He said he had picked the place at random but I had a queer feeling, since it was not his kind of place, he had gone there on purpose. I thought he didn't want anybody to see me with him, and since no one we know patronizes that kind of place it would be safe. . . . Anyhow they fixed us some dinner quite nicely and gave us good drinks. I told him that Nancy was to have an uncontested divorce pronto, or else."

"Or else what?"

"That is what I can't tell you. Not yet. He argued. But I sat tight. And he finally gave in. He promised. I stayed with him till he phoned Nancy. Then I had to run for the one o'clock train which was the last which could get me back in Los Angeles at the approximate time Rufus would be expecting me from San Diego."

"What time did you leave Leland?" Patrick asked.

"I know exactly. At ten minutes to one."

"He was killed—or rather his car went down the hill—at approximately one-twenty. He had thirty minutes to live after you left him."

Helen Moore shivered.

"I'll tell you why it was so urgent that he and Nancy divorce at once, Mr. Abbott. Gwen Telfer is after Phil Hannegan. She'll get him—or she would have—if Nancy weren't free."

"I don't agree with you there," Patrick said.

"You don't know Gwen," Helen answered. "I've known her all my life."

I stared at her. This was getting very interesting.

But she didn't say any more then.

"Look, I've got to run. I'll be missed, and Rufus will get hectic and phone the police, and then—you can imagine!"

She turned toward the door.

The house phone buzzed. Patrick took it. He suggested that somebody wait downstairs. He hung up. He said, "I'll see you home, Helen. Please wait here."

"Please don't trouble."

"It's no trouble. But there's somebody downstairs I've got to send away first. . . . Oh, oh," he said then, as we heard the elevator cage stop at our floor. "Listen, when I open the front door, slip out this way and wait for me on the service stairs. I won't be long. But don't go home alone, Helen. I don't want to alarm you, but I think you're in serious danger."

The doorbell was ringing, one prolonged ring as a finger pressed continuously on the bell. Patrick went off into the hall. He opened the door. I could hear Gwen's clear voice. Helen murmured speaking-of-the-devil and opened the back door. "Tell Pat not to bother. I'll be quite safe," she said, and slipped out. I locked the door after her.

ELEVEN

Patrick was having rather a time getting rid of Gwen. I could hear her talking. The lift in her voice suggested that she was arguing. Pretending that I needed to fix up my face, but really to hear better what was being said in the entry, I went from the kitchen to our bedroom.

Promptly I lost interest in the conversation at the door, because as I switched on the lights I saw my bag lying open on the dressing table with its contents spilling out. On the floor beside the open closet door lay my best new shoes. This was most peculiar, because I still kept them in their box.

I checked over the stuff from my bag. All that was missing—unless some small change had been taken from the change purse—was a sheaf of postage stamps.

A ten-dollar bill, two fives, and three ones were safe in the zippered compartment.

I closed the bag and picked up the shoes. I couldn't find their box.

Patrick came in.

"Come along, Jeanie. We're going to see that waiter."

"Waiter? The one in the Mexican joint? What about Gwen?"

"Gwen is downstairs with a cab. You go down and keep her interested while I sneak Helen out the back way. I want to take her home."

"Why?"

"She shouldn't have come out in the first place. Keep Gwen. We need her cab."

"Helen's gone," I said. "She wouldn't wait. She must be home by now."

Patrick said something violent about Gwen Telfer.

"Pat, somebody's frisked my bag. And they've only taken stamps, and a shoebox."

Patrick gave me one look, then streaked for the maid's room. Chris Leland was gone! The bed was even made up, though not too well, which would indicate that he wasn't coming back.

"We had a hard time getting a client in this case, and then we couldn't keep him," I said.

"No cracks," Patrick said. "Come along."

"What are we going to do?"

"I told you. We're going to see that waiter. Gwen is going with us for the pure and simple reason that she's got a taxi. I want you to keep Gwen in the cab while I go into that joint and look around."

We were back in the kitchen. Patrick unlocked the service door I had locked when Helen went out. Chris had unlocked it to go out, which was why it wasn't locked when Helen Moore arrived. Chris must have left it open in case he had to come back, Patrick said. We would leave the door ready, in case he did, he said. I said this apartment tonight was like the Grand Central Station. Patrick was not amused.

"I wish Helen had waited for me," Patrick said again.

"Maybe she wasn't going directly home," I said.

"Maybe."

"Why did Gwen come here, Pat?"

"Checking up on me, apparently."

"Does she know you really aren't working for Nancy?"

"I'm afraid she suspects it. Come on. Don't let her pump you, by the way. If any pumping's done, you do it, Jean."

"Maybe she killed him herself," I said.

"Motive?" Patrick snapped, hurrying me along the hall. "Gwen's not the type to murder a golden-egg goose."

I said, "What do you make of that missing shoebox . . . ?"

Patrick said, "I think Chris wanted to get rid of the gun. He put it in your shoebox, wrapped it, addressed it, and stuck your stamps on it."

"You should have taken his gun, Pat."

"I guess you're right."

Gwendolyn Telfer was pacing the lobby. Her jewel-eyes were snapping and her smartly painted lips were drawn up in a hard little circle.

"I thought you were never coming!" she greeted us.

"And I hope you haven't let that cab get away!" Patrick said, in exactly the same annoyed tone.

"Of course he's *not* got away. But do I have to go and sit out there in the rain while your wife primps . . ."

"Leave my wife out of this!" Patrick said, with mock bravado.

Even Gwen managed a tiny smile. She said, "This man here," and she wagged a finger at Vincent Smith, "says young Chris Leland has been hanging around up here tonight. Why?"

"Didn't he tell you?" Patrick said. "Come on, gals. Let's scram."

Vincent trotted ahead and opened the door for us. Obviously Gwen had oiled his willing palm.

The fog had now turned into a gray drizzle. Gwen popped into the cab first. I followed her in and Patrick told the driver where to take us. "Go down Leavenworth to Union," he said. I was glad we would be avoiding that Jones Street hill. We sat in the close hushed interior. The windows were clouded over. We said very little in the short interval which passed before the cab rolled up on Broadway near Powell. Patrick got out and walked away in the direction of the Mexican place.

"Now what's he up to?" Gwen asked.

"I've no idea," I said.

He was back in a very short time. He spoke to the driver and our next stop was Police Headquarters on Kearny Street.

"I won't be a minute," he said.

"I'm coming in with you," Gwen said.

"If you do I won't go in," Patrick said.

Gwen was angry. "You won't double-cross me, will you, Pat? You'll urge them to go after Chris, won't you?"

Patrick said, "If you want to be dead sure, Gwennie, go ahead and do it yourself. But I won't go in with you."

"Oh, bother!" Gwen cried. "Beat it before I explode, you!"

When he had left us, she said, "I don't see how you put up with him. He is the most obstinate human being I ever met."

"I don't find him so at all," I said. Untruthfully, but I certainly wouldn't be caught agreeing with her on *that* subject.

Gwen squirmed. The interior of the cab was vibrant from her petulance. "I'm only trying to help. I sense things, Jean, which probably sounds like foolishness to you, but it's the truth. It isn't that I have any sixth sense or anything, but I am so in the habit of dealing with people that I do have a superior sort of insight into things. Your wits get sharpened. I sat there at home tonight and thought that the way to solve this business was to come and get Pat and go right to work and keep right on the job till it's finished. But why was he so mysterious, there at your place? He wouldn't even let me come in, made me wait downstairs. Is that Leland boy really up there, the way that porter thought?"

"No," I said, truthfully.

"That Vincent Smith thinks so."

"He'll probably go in and look, while we're out," I said. "I think he's like that. He'll be disappointed."

"I frankly don't think Pat's efficient," Gwen said.

"Pat's very efficient," I said. "He wouldn't get anywhere at all, though, if he zoomed around the way efficient people do in business. Nothing personal intended, Gwen."

"Well, you needn't get sore," Gwen said. "I was just speaking my mind."

Gwen got out her cigarettes and offered me one somewhat grudgingly. She lit both with her lighter.

Her crisp voice opened a fresh offensive.

"Well, Pat doesn't run his show the way I would, anyway. I wouldn't rest till I had run down every clue. I'd have that boy in jail by this time, and I don't mean maybe. I would be ruthless, and persistent as hell."

You certainly would, I was thinking.

"I could show Pat a few tricks," Gwen said. "If he doesn't step up his methods, Jean, you'll never get any further than pennies in the piggy bank, and no kidding."

"Wouldn't that be just awful!" I said, sarcastically.

"Well, what do people work for?" Gwen demanded. She answered it herself. "Money. The faster you work the more money you get. Pat's slow."

"You don't know him, Gwen."

"I've known him longer than you, Jean."

"You don't really know him. I'm married to him, and I don't know sometimes if he's working or not . . ."

"I would know, if I were married to him. . . ."

"You'd never be married to him, Gwen. He wouldn't marry a woman who tried to run his life."

"Oh, hell!" Gwen said.

I knew I had got under her skin, and I was sorry. I didn't want to sit in the close confines of the cab and quarrel with her or anybody. Also, if we got in a quarrel I was afraid Gwen Telfer would win.

Patrick had said to pump her. I did some fast thinking.

Chris had robbed my bag, if only of a few stamps, and he had walked out on our hospitality. Maybe she was partially right about the boy. His inheritance couldn't be so hot on his father's side, either, if Helen Moore and Philip Hannegan were right in their estimates of Ernest Leland.

"What makes you so positive it was Chris?" I asked.

Gwen said, "Who else could it be? Nobody either loved or hated Ernest Leland very much. Nobody that knew him, I mean. If the kid had really known him he wouldn't've hated him. But he didn't know him. It was only in his mind that he hated his father. That's why he could come out here and murder him, see."

"That's interesting," I said. "I'd got the idea you admired Ernest Leland tremendously?"

"Oh, I did," said Gwen. "He was a prince."

"He sounds cold as a fish," I said.

"He was," Gwen said. "He got and did what he wanted. He never let sentiment stand in his way."

My God, I thought, not at the revelation of Leland's character, which I had heard before, of course, but because of her profound admiration of it.

"I knew him better than anyone," Gwen said. "When I came to the city I was a raw gal, and no kidding, but by a slick piece of luck my first job was a typing job for Ernest Leland, a report of some kind on some oil property he owned. He liked my work and continued to throw things my way. Pretty soon he heard of a good opening in an advertising agency and got me into it. I work. Ernest never regretted anything he did for me. I handed it back in one way or another, all polished up and paying pretty dividends. We got on fine. I'll miss him."

"Were you fond of him, Gwen?"

"In a way. Naturally."

"You handled all the advertising of all Leland products, didn't you?"

"Practically speaking," Gwen said. She enumerated a few. Wines. A candy. A soap. A list of cereals in which he was heavily invested. And others.

"What was he like, really?" I asked, again.

"Ernest? He was tops."

"What do you mean by that?"

"Well, he was keen, clever. Always one jump ahead of anybody else. He got a great big kick out of putting over a fast one."

She hadn't told me a thing. I said, "Did he really love Nancy, do you think?"

Gwen fidgeted again. "Of course he did. Naturally, a man like that doesn't let a woman dominate his entire life. But who wants that? Nobody but a silly sort of hen. Nancy never objected to his having thousands of other interests besides herself. At least so far as I know. She was a fool to leave him. My goodness, he gave her everything, and she could go her own way absolutely without his giving a damn. But at the same time he didn't want her to divorce him. It would humiliate him. The way anything that flopped always did."

"Gwen," I said, repelled, "he still sounds to me like a very cold fish."

"Well, maybe he was. People have to be cold to get anywhere."

I was not getting anywhere. I looked ahead along the dim street at some blinking neons, felt Gwen being restless beside me.

I took another tack.

"Did you really and truly like him, Gwen?" I persisted.

"Sure, I liked him. He was swell."

"Do you like Nancy?"

Gwen was slower on that uptake. "Sure. Why not?"

"Helen Moore is beautiful, don't you think?"

"Beautiful?" Gwen snapped. "She's well got up, you mean."

"Have you known her long?"

"Pretty long," Gwen said drily.

"I think she's charming," I babbled. "Such a wonderful smile and all. And her clothes!" Gwen was being silent. "I don't think she's more than twenty-four, do you, Gwen?"

Gwen, the astute, fell for that old one like bricks. "She's thirty."

"I'd have to see a birth certificate to believe that, Gwen."

Gwen said, "I've know Helen all her life. I knew her during the Hollywood *Elaine* period. She couldn't make that grade in ten thousand years. She's a type, nothing more, and there's at least a million just like her with her same idea, and, by now, considerably less years. She never had a chance."

"Oh. It must be very disappointing to fail as a movie actress. I mean, it all happens and is over with when you're so young."

"She finally landed all right," Gwen sniffed. "She likes what she's got."

"I guess so. She seems absolutely devoted to Rufus."

"Apparently. But maybe she learned to act well enough to fool *him*," Gwen said. "Rufus is a dumb bunny that owes his present good job to his sister's marrying the boss. Ernest introduced Helen to Rufus, by the way. I often wonder if it wasn't one way for him to get rid of Helen, or Elaine as she was at that period, since she certainly wasn't paying off."

"You mean, he backed her?"

Gwen said, "Well, to be perfectly honest, I don't know if he did or not. I do know he knew her for a good while before she married Rufus Moore. Somebody had to fork out for her ravishing wardrobe, and she couldn't've done it out of the peanuts she made out of an occasional small part. She says her mother bought her clothes. I'd like to know how, unless mama struck oil or something after I lost touch with them. Helen came from a family on the wrong side of the tracks, just like mine. We're both from near Fresno originally. Helen was a pretty kid and her mother went without everything to save up and take her to Hollywood when she was seventeen, the way they all do. I introduced Ernest Leland to them myself, once when we met them by chance in Los Angeles. I do know that from that day on Helen's wardrobe picked up, but her parts in pictures got worse and worse just the same. Somebody paid for her clothes and it wasn't Helen. What of it? Maybe she was one of Ernest's investments that didn't pay off. He never talked about his mistakes. See here, I'm talking too much. It's because I'm mad. I'm going after Pat."

She had opened the door and was stepping out when Patrick dashed down the wide stone steps, told her to get back in, and gave the cab driver an address. "Drive like hell!" he said. He pushed Gwen back into her seat and jumped in and slammed the door.

"Why, that was Nancy Leland's number you gave him!" Gwen said, as the driver was turning around.

"Bright girl, Gwennie," Patrick said.

"What's happened?" I asked.

He did not reply for a moment. Then he said, "There's been another murder, and this one happened inside the house."

TWELVE

The cab turned into Union Street and shot up the first lap of the hill. The fog in the rain thickened. We sat in the lightless interior hearing the tires sucking at the wet pavements.

Gwen Telfer said, "Who is it?"

"I don't know," Patrick said.

She was cross again. How aware of her you always were. There she sat, small in her corner of the cab. She made no actual physical contact with anyone. I sat in my corner. Patrick was sitting sideways on one of the folding seats.

Gwen's annoyance was the most definite thing in the cab. The air prickled with it.

"Why didn't you ask?" Gwen said.

"I was in a hurry," said Patrick.

"Who found her?" Gwen asked then.

Patrick said, "What makes you think it was a her?"

"You just said so."

"I didn't."

Gwen breathed audibly. "How did you know about it, by the way?"

"I happened to be in the Inspector's office when the news came over their radio. I didn't wait for any details. I want to get there ahead of the police."

Gwen leaned forward. "Why?"

"A clever gal like you ought to realize that it is always a help to get anywhere first."

"I wish you wouldn't try to be so amusing," Gwen said.

"Okay," Patrick said.

Gwen waited a moment, then said, "Why did you go down to the police station anyway, Pat?"

"I went to visit the morgue."

"Morgue?" She sat back. Her voice hummed with her scorn. "Look, darling, Ernest Leland's body was removed to a mortician's the minute

I knew about his death. I took care of that. Far be it from me to run your business, but—well, really, Pat!"

Patrick said amiably, "Maybe you could put me on a paying basis, Gwennie."

"Shut up!"

The cab turned left up that tilted block on Jones Street. The driver changed to low gear. The motor screamed as if with agony and once or twice the wheels whirled impotently against the wet concrete.

Patrick said, "Gwen, so help me, if you start showing off at Nancy's, I'll have you tossed out on your ear. You're coming back with us right now only because it would have taken time to throw you out there at the police station. I had to have this cab. See? Now shut up and behave yourself and maybe the police will be impressed and hire you to show the force how to become efficient."

He tapped on the glass. The driver swung over to the curb directly in front of Nancy's house. Gwen kept still. Frozen, in her own wrath.

The house was a shadow, blurred in the rain. The lamps outside the door were white blurs.

Patrick was opening the unlocked front door before I was halfway up the walk. For once in her life Gwen Telfer brought up the rear.

Helen Moore was stretched face downward in a welter of dark, glistening blood. She was lying in the main hall just inside the open door from the entry. Her face lay in profile. She was wearing what we had last seen her in, the gray flannel dress and the tweed coat which was probably her husband's.

Nancy Leland was leaning against the railing halfway up the stairs. Mary Wong stood between the body and the door under the stairs which opened into the service hall. The lights were full on.

At such a moment it is queer the things you notice. I saw the dark splotch on Nancy's white forearm before I noticed that she wore a red housecoat. There was a pencil of light from somewhere lying across the front of Mary Wong's dead-black dress, just below her twisting yellow hands. Nancy looked composed. Mary Wong was a picture of restrained grief. Her thin little body drooped and tears glistened in her black screwed-up eyes.

There was utter silence as Patrick stooped beside the dead woman. Only I among those present could have sensed his remorse. I knew he was asking himself why—oh, why—hadn't he brought her home. He had warned her that she might be in danger. He had told her to wait until he could see her back to this house. But Gwen—busybody Gwen—had prevented it.

Well, Helen had come on before Patrick could accompany her, and of her own accord. She didn't want him with her, perhaps. Gwen was not to blame. It was just one of those things, a fatal sequence of thises and thats a series of blunders, nobody's fault in particular, all leading step by step to murder.

For that matter you might say it was Helen's own fault for leaving this house. But I knew that Patrick was chastening himself.

Patrick felt a wrist, touched the white forehead, took out a pencil from his vest pocket and drew it through the blood. It made a wake, which closed slowly, leaving no trace. He laid the pencil on the carpet beside the body.

Gwen Telfer stood near me. We were still in the entry. She stood stiff as a poker. Her face was white, her turquoise eyes glassy. She stared as if hypnotized at the body of Helen Moore.

Patrick stood up. "Who did it, Nancy?" he asked.

Nancy Leland said, from the stairs, "Oh, Pat! I don't know! I heard the shot and came down and found her."

"You got here at once?"

"No-o. It took a moment to think what the noise was. So often cars backfire on the hill. I lay there slowly realizing that the noise was inside this house. I got up and put on my housecoat and came down. I saw her lying there and ran to the phone and called the police."

Patrick said, "There is blood on your arm, Nancy."

Nancy said, "Well, I touched her. I tried to move her, turn her face so she could breathe—there was so much blood—it came—throbbing..."

"Where is Rufus?"

"We just couldn't bring ourselves to wake him," Nancy said.

Patrick said, "You roused Mary Wong, didn't you, before you called the police?"

"Why, yes," Nancy said.

Patrick said, "The police will be arriving at any time, Nancy. You'd better get your story straight, each part of it in the right order. From the condition of the blood Helen Moore has been dead at least twenty minutes."

Nancy said, "The shot woke me. I lay a moment thinking. I put on my coat and came into the hall. There is a second light switch for the hall lights up here. I turned on the lights and saw Helen lying there, when I got about this far down the stairs. I recognized her by her hair. I hurried down and tried to lift her head. Blood was spurting from her throat. I knew she hadn't a chance. I ran back upstairs and across the passage to call Mary. Then I went to the phone in the study off the living room and called the police."

"Did you find the gun?"

Nancy shook her head.

Patrick's eyes were busy. He suddenly dipped and, taking the handkerchief from his breast pocket, picked up something from under the edge of the tweed coat. He stuffed handkerchief and all in his raincoat pocket.

Gwen Telfer came out of her trance.

"Did you call a doctor, Nancy?" she asked.

"No—I didn't."

"Why not? That's a natural thing to do," said Gwen.

"Our doctor lives some distance away, and it's such an awful night, and Mary agreed that Helen was dead, so . . ."

"Better call him," Patrick said. "Good thing to have the doctor here, Nancy."

Nancy suddenly gripped the railing. "I—I can't."

"You call him," Patrick said to Gwen Telfer.

"All right," Gwen said, but reluctantly. "But, look, Pat, you've got to coach Nancy, hear? She's already in a spot because of Ernest, and now this. I don't think she ought to say anything at all. I think she ought to call my lawyer."

"The doctor first," Patrick said. "Give Gwen his number, Nancy."

"I know the damn number, Pat. I use the same doctor. But, look, the important thing is coaching Nancy so she won't give the show away. She had a perfect motive for killing Ernest, and everybody knows she has a brother complex and she didn't like Helen . . ."

"Gwen," Nancy said, from the stairs, "you really are wonderful. You—really—are."

"My dear! Just be sensible for once. Policemen are a motley crew. No telling what they'll dream up about you before they're finished. Ernest is bound to have a lot of relations who will pop up now like mushrooms claiming his money, and even if they can't put you in San Quentin they will leave you without one thin dime . . ."

"Gwen," Patrick said, "go call the doctor!"

Grumbling, Gwen marched off towards the study.

Patrick turned to Mary Wong. "Did you dress after Mrs. Leland called you? Or hadn't you yet undressed?"

Nancy answered. "She always dresses when we call her in the night. It's habit. My father was ill so long."

"You went for her, Nancy? You didn't ring instead?"

"I went. It was all I could think to do somehow."

"You didn't hear the gunshot, Mary?"

Nancy answered for her again. "Of course she didn't hear it. There are two walls and a stretch of outdoors between her bedroom and this hall."

Patrick said, "Let Mary do her own talking, Nancy."

Mary spoke, in her flat voice. "It is as Miss Nancy says."

Patrick said, "Where were you sleeping, Nancy?"

"In my own room. The door straight ahead at the top of these stairs. I was the closest, the one most likely to hear any noise down here."

"And Rufus?"

"He's at the far end of the hall, the furthest room of all from here. Helen slept in father's room. There is a bath which connects those two rooms. Helen took one of our two phones to her room. She asked to sleep alone because her mother is very ill and she was going to try to call her in the night, or rather leave word down there that she could be reached here. You know how long it sometimes takes long-distance calls to come through now and Helen didn't want Rufus disturbed. Rufus was so upset. I think he took sleeping capsules to make sure he'd sleep."

"What's the matter with her mother?"

"I don't know," Nancy said.

"Well, I know," Gwen said, coming back. "She is a morphine addict. She's dying of it."

Nancy gasped. "Oh, Gwen! How can you . . . ?"

"Don't tell me you didn't know that?"

"I didn't. And I don't believe it."

"Well, it's true. Helen was mortally ashamed of it, of course, and did everything on earth to keep it quiet. I guess that was why her mother moved down to San Diego, away from anybody they knew. Mrs. Bishop always did everything Helen wanted her to, so I suppose she moved off to die alone when she was told to. There's no harm in telling it all now. She's about finished, and Helen was her only child, and Mr. Bishop is dead, too."

"It can still hurt Rufus," Nancy said.

"Oh, fie! Everything is going to be aired now. Everything will be in the papers. Every little thing will be pried into. They even went to my milliner about that pink feather hat." I saw Nancy's fingers tighten on the railing. "They swore her not to tell, but of course I'm a good customer and she rang me right up and said they asked all sorts of questions about the hat."

Gwen gazed with a kind of wonder at Nancy's monumental capacity for blundering. She said, under her breath, as if the colossal dumbness of Nancy Leland had suddenly struck her, "Jesus Christ!"

Patrick said, "Someone must go and tell Rufus."

Nancy gripped the railing. The Chinese woman gave a slight negative jerk of her head.

"I'd better go myself," Patrick said. "While I'm upstairs stay just as you are. Don't move and don't touch anything, remember." He spoke to me. "Come inside the hall, Jeanie, and stand near the foot of the stairs."

He went up the steps two and three at a time.

There was a silence, a waiting. The big clock at the other end of the hall ticked. Gwen looked at her watch. If the police always took all this time she would certainly advise against getting murdered, she said. I said they were terribly short of men. She said it was just bad management.

We listened then to quick oddly uneven footsteps on the walk. The door swung open, and Philip Hannegan came in. His glance swept past the woman on the floor until it met Nancy's. He moved into the hall, watching Nancy only, as if he were unaware of anyone else in the place. Out of my eye corners I looked at Gwen Telfer. She was watching those two with a peculiar intentness. Her expression made me shudder.

THIRTEEN

Gwen spoke up. "I warned you not to come here, Phil." There was real anxiety in her voice. "You'd better go away now, before the police come."

Philip Hannegan did not answer. He stood beside the staircase looking up at Nancy Leland. He asked what he could do. He made no move to touch her. But it was all there, in her eyes, in his, and I was frightened for them.

Gwen took a step forward and said furiously, "For God's sake, Phil! Get out! Why on earth do you think I telephoned you? This is no place for you."

Nancy looked at Gwen. Her face became sphinxlike. Was she thinking, as I was, about why Gwen kept mixing up in this affair? Did she think there was something completely shameless in Gwen's curiosity and busybodiness? Was she wondering if Gwen herself hadn't done these frightful murders, and if so, why? Had those two people, Ernest Leland and Helen Moore, stood, for some reason, in Gwen Telfer's way?

What did Patrick think?

He had told me nothing at all. He seldom told me everything, alas, till he got good and ready, but this time I felt particularly left out.

Also, he never deliberately exposed me to real danger. I got into trouble sometimes, but it was usually my own fault. Therefore, if he thought Gwen a murderess, would he have left me alone with her in that cab? Still, there couldn't have been a safer place, because, except for a very few minutes, we had sat in the cab in front of the police headquarters. The driver had never left us alone together. Patrick was constantly expected to return.... But how could Gwen have murdered Helen Moore? Impossible! Helen was still in our kitchen while Gwen was at the front door talking to Patrick. Helen had slipped away while they talked and had made her way home. Had she gone home directly? No.... Gwen could not have killed Helen Moore. Even if she had seen her leave, had trailed and shot her, she could hardly have got back downstairs by the time we came down. . . . Well, perhaps. If everything clicked just right. But, wait, Gwen had been talking with our elevator man in the lobby while we got ready to go in her cab to the police station. Her clothes had not been damp from the fog, as they would have been had she been outside while we lingered upstairs. . . . *You can kill by deputy.* . . . Gwen certainly would not do the job herself. That would not be truly efficient. . . .

I slipped Gwen a look, standing there, so neatly packaged, as she might say of one of the products she advertised. Her eyes were glimmering with fury over what she had seen in Philip Hannegan's face when he looked at Nancy Leland. What would she do now?

Patrick came back downstairs. He was glad to see Philip Hannegan.

"I can't rouse Rufus," he said. "Suppose you try it, Phil. How many of those capsules did he take, Nancy?"

Nancy said, "There were a dozen I'd just had by prescription . . ."

"There are nine there. If he's had only three we can wake him, all right." Phil had already started upstairs. "Be with you in a minute," Patrick said. "They're coming now."

Inspector Sam Bradish entered at the head of a band of experts and policemen, some in uniform, some not. His head was down and his big shoulders hunched. His sparkling eyes took in the scene. He walked around the body and halted, facing Patrick. "You'll have a sweet time explaining this, baby!" he growled, and then got on with the job with a minimum of fuss. The policemen were painstakingly scattered. The experts went to work. The family doctor arrived and went into a huddle beside the body with the police surgeon. I listened to their formal palaver. It was as impersonal as though Helen Moore had been an anonymous body lying on the street. Death was due to a gunshot wound undoubtedly, though there was no gun in sight and no bullet. They sniffed and remarked that there was still a lingering aroma of cordite. The carotid artery had been ripped open in the throat. She must have died almost instantly and with the minimum of pain. No tattooing on the skin, which would indicate that the shot was fired from a distance of at least six feet. They dragged that same pencil through the blood and watched it slowly smooth out the wake. Dead less than an hour. An autopsy was, they agreed, indicated.

A police stenographer wrote down everything anybody said.

"I want the women out of here. Go into that living room," Bradish said. "You, too," he directed Mary Wong.

I looked up at Nancy Leland. She was grasping the railing tightly as though she dared not let go. I ran up to lend her an arm. She kept shaking like a leaf all the way to the living room. I walked her over to one of the sofas. The fire was dead. The room had a fetid smell, from last evening's cigarette smoke. Mary Wong came in and went at once to the fireplace and started the fire with kindling from a basket on the hearth. I suggested a drink for Nancy, and when she nodded, got her a glass of whisky from the portable bar. She had it in her hand when Gwen Telfer came in.

"Don't touch that!" Gwen ordered.

Nancy lifted the glass and drank it straight.

"You are a fool!" Gwen cried out. "What will the police think?"

"I'll say I forced the liquor on her," I said.

Gwen said, "Go to the kitchen and make some coffee and tea, Mary."

The Chinese woman was putting a log on the fire. She straightened up and turned to Nancy for confirmation of Gwen's command. Nancy shook her head.

"Do as I say!" Gwen cried.

Nancy said, "The Inspector said we were to stay here. Sit down, Mary." The Chinese woman bowed, crossed to the end of the room where a door led into the back hall, and seated herself on a straight chair. Gwen walked over to the mantel and stood there, striking it small angry blows with her manicured fist.

"I have something to say to you, Nancy," Gwen said. "But first I want Mary out of this room. And Jean, too."

"They're both staying," Nancy said.

Gwen's eyes looked dangerous.

"Okay. You asked for it, see. Did you know that Helen went to see Philip Hannegan tonight?"

"No, I didn't know it," Nancy said.

"Helen knew something," Gwen declared. "She paid for it with her life."

Nancy made no answer.

"I phoned Phil just now to try to stop him coming over here," Gwen said. "When I went to call the doctor I called Phil first. I told him what had happened. He said he would be right down. I told him not to come, not to get mixed up in this. I told him that was my reason for calling him. I was afraid he might hear the police sirens and blunder down here and maybe talk himself into a bad spot. He said that Helen had tried to see him tonight and that he felt he must come because he had not seen her long enough to know just why she wanted to talk to him and he felt somehow that her death was partly his fault. That's ridiculous. Now he's come here and unless we are all very careful he'll get frightfully involved. He's just getting started back on his career and he absolutely must not be dragged into this mess."

I said, "Phil looks as if he can take it."

"I—won't—have—it!" Gwen stormed.

Nancy said, "I want another drink, Jean. Should I take it?"

"Why not?" I said. I got up and poured her another smallish one and got one for myself. The whisky was already picking her up. Her cheeks were pinkening. Her tousled dark hair fell about her face as charmingly as though she had had the time to arrange it. The warm red housecoat became her.

Gwen doubled one fist and stood striking the other cupped palm with it.

"I haven't put all my cards on the table, Nancy," she said.

Nancy said, "That's too bad."

Gwen said, "You think you've been making a fool of me, don't you, Nancy? You think it's funny, I suppose, that all the time I've been trying to help you, you've been carrying on with Phil behind my back."

The faintest of smiles curved Nancy's red lips for a fleeting instant. She made no reply.

Gwen, goaded by her silence, stamped her foot.

Then she cast a look at Mary Wong, a darker shadow in the shadowed end of the big room.

"Send her out of here!" she said.

Mary Wong rose and said, in her flat but dignified voice, "I could wait just outside in the hall, Miss Nancy."

Nancy said, "All right. Don't go anywhere but the hall, Mary. Every move we make they'll think suspicious."

The Chinese woman bowed and went out the door near where she had been sitting and closed it quietly but definitely.

"I'll make a deal with you," Gwen said. "I didn't want to say my say before that woman, though. I never trust Orientals. I don't like talking before Jean, either, but I guess she knows which side her bread is buttered on, and won't make us any trouble. After all, Pat's working for you, after a fashion, and if he's careful and my lawyer is as good as usual we'll get you out of this. In return, you're to lay off Phil Hannegan."

Nancy's eyes widened with a sort of admiration. She did not speak.

Gwen continued, "That hat can hang you, Nancy. Who but you could have left it in the car? Well, that's no concern of mine. Let's say you killed Ernest, and then you killed Helen because she guessed the truth. She knew him better than any of us. Better than I did, even, I suspect. That's none of my business either. A gal has to get on in this world. Okay, I'm offering you your life, Nancy, and here is how it can be done.

"That pink hat is a duplicate of a blue one I bought two weeks before Ernest Leland went to Mexico on this last trip. I called up Madeleine about them tonight. Both are entered to my account but there is no entry about the color of either hat. One is entered merely as a feather hat, purchased a month ago. The other as a feather hat purchased ten days ago. Now, I had dinner at Cliff House with Ernest Leland a day or two before he went to Mexico. I wore my blue feather hat. I left it in his car when we went in to dinner. There is no one who could swear that I had on a blue hat that evening. So I shall say it was the pink hat and that I forgot it that night in his car. Then he went away and I didn't know where to find the hat so I bought another, a blue one this time. Madeleine—my milliner—is very susceptible to money. I can fix her all right. She will tell the police she was mistaken in thinking the pink hat was bought for you. She will say I bought the pink hat first and the blue hat second."

I said, "Gwen, you're nuts! Dozens of people will have seen the blue hat . . ."

"They are not important," Gwen said.

"You are crazy!" I said.

"I am not. When other people say blue I merely say pink, and stick to it. You'd be surprised how people give in if you'll stay definite. You two will have to be definite, too. People will soon be saying we are right. Madeleine is a certainty. She will do what I say. Did many people see you wear the pink hat, Nancy?"

"No-o," Nancy said.

"That's fine!" Gwen said. "Then it's a deal?"

Nancy laughed ruefully. "Gwen, you really are amazing," she said. "But how can you hope to get away with a thing like that?"

"Look, there's no time. You're to do as I say, that's all."

Gwen had regained her poise. She moved a little way from the increasingly hot fire. Her precise admirable figure was limned against the flames. "Now, listen. All you do is sit tight. Don't answer anything. The lawyer will think up the answers. I'm going to ask that Inspector right away for permission to telephone him. In return, you lay off Phil, see? Forever. . . . And also you are to do nothing to interfere with the Leland advertising accounts. You will inherit and theoretically take Ernest's place in the management of the business and our agency interests are to stay just as they were. You'll never regret it, Nancy. Is that all clear?"

"Perfectly clear," Nancy said.

I gave Nancy a slanting glance and was astonished to see that her entire expression had changed, that she seemed to be considering Gwen's crazy proposition sincerely.

"You won't be sorry, Nancy. It will also mean that Rufus can keep his job, of course."

Nancy sighed.

"I'm afraid he won't care much about his job now."

"Yes, he will. I don't say he won't be all shot, he will be, but we can fix up some sort of good break for him, somehow, among us, and he will snap out of it in due time. Hey, you don't suppose that Chink is listening at the keyhole?"

Nancy winced. "No, she isn't," she said.

"You seem very sure!"

"Yes, I'm sure. Mary never did a contemptible thing in her life. She is pure undefiled goodness."

Gwen twisted impatiently.

There were footsteps in the front hall.

"Okay. Listen, someone is coming—remember—just sit tight . . ."

"Gwen, you are stark staring crazy!" I said.

"Shut up!" Gwen said. "You're in it already up to your neck. Pat hasn't a leg to stand on." She dropped to a whisper. "By the way, Chris Leland is our ace in the hole, remember. They'll round him up. They'll arrest him. I'm their witness, of course. They probably won't be able to convict him. If they do, at his age, it only means a few years." She spoke softly, as she added, "It isn't as though you didn't do it, Nancy. You did do it, you know."

Nancy did not answer. She sat looking at Gwen as though mesmerized by the brilliant, exquisitely set blue eyes.

FOURTEEN

Inspector Bradish had his stenographer pull up a table to a spot which dominated the room, and which was away from the fireplace and near the opposite ends of the two sofas. Rufus Moore was put in a chair on his right. The light fell mercilessly on his greenish unhappy face. He did not seem quite awake. Gwen—who had got permission from Inspector Bradish to call her lawyer but had not yet reached him—took a seat next to Nancy as if to guard her against saying the wrong thing. Mary Wong had returned to the room. She sat slightly in the shadows and behind Nancy Leland. I sat facing Nancy, and Philip Hannegan was on my right and Patrick back of us.

Bradish started establishing alibis. Again, it was Nancy who was vulnerable. Even the sleeping tablets had been given Rufus by Nancy. Why? Because he was worried and upset, she said, and he said the same thing. Bradish scoffed at it.

"I half believe you're both in it together," he said.

"Why should we want to kill Helen?" Nancy asked.

"Maybe she knew too much," answered Bradish.

Gwen said, "If you knew how devoted Rufus Moore was to his wife you couldn't even imagine such a thing, Inspector Bradish."

Bradish said, "Well, if she goes out and runs around in the dark at a time like this maybe she asked for it." He glared at Nancy. "Why did she leave this house?"

"Don't answer," Gwen said.

"I couldn't," Nancy said. "I don't know why she left the house."

Philip Hannegan leaned forward to speak. But Patrick beat him to it. "She came to see me," he said.

Philip gave him a startled glance, and sat back.

"You?" Bradish said. "Why?"

"She thought I might be able to help Nancy Leland, Sam."

"A lot of people seem to have had that idea," Bradish said drily.

Rufus spoke thickly, from drowsiness and nausea, "Helen was terribly worried for my poor sister. That could explain her going out alone to see Pat. . . ."

"Just why did she come?" Bradish asked Patrick.

"Sam, will you make me a Deputy Inspector for a couple of hours?"

Bradish said, "What are you up to anyhow, Abbott? And, by the way, why did you go to the morgue?"

"The usual reason. To look at a dead man."

Rufus was blundering ahead. He had been talking all the time. ". . . My sister does not realize that anyone could even think she is guilty. She is so young. But Helen sensed that once she was suspected of murder she would always be under a cloud. Specially if the real murderer is not apprehended . . ."

"The murderer will be caught, Mr. Moore," Bradish said. "What dead man, Pat? Did you think Leland's body was still in the morgue?"

"Yes, he did," Gwen Telfer put in aptly. "If he had told me why he was going to police headquarters I could have saved him the trip, Inspector. I knew the body had been taken away."

"Will you do what I asked, Sam?"

"No," Bradish said to Patrick. He turned back to Nancy. "And you did not hear your sister-in-law leave the house? She had to pass your door, you know, come downstairs, go out the front door. It's a heavy door. She must have made some noise."

"I did not hear her go," Nancy said. "Or return."

"What about you?" Bradish said to Mary Wong.

Nancy started to speak up. Gwen nudged her.

But as Mary answered Bradish I was conscious, as Bradish was, too, of Nancy's sharp uneasiness. She did not even breathe until Mary Wong said, in her flat voice, "I heard nothing."

"You're all lying," Bradish said. He addressed Mary Wong. "Don't be a fool! Tell what you know. You've got a good reputation. We've checked on you, see. We know all about you. We know about your family, good girls, all of them. Well educated. How will they feel if you go to jail?"

Nancy cried out, as Gwen nudged her discreetly, "That's ridiculous!"

"Okay," Bradish said, pleased with what looked like progress. "You know what will happen to you if you lie to protect Mrs. Leland, Mary? It makes you guilty, too. You will be punished, put in prison."

"I know nothing," Mary Wong said, but her lips trembled, and Nancy's fright was there for anybody to see. Bradish's eyes were dancing. He had found a weak spot, Mary Wong.

It would take time to wear them down. I felt most unhappy. Patrick and I would have to tell Bradish everything we knew, too. Patrick had been holding out on them for Nancy's sake.

Surely Nancy was guilty, at least to some extent. She was certainly concealing important evidence. Why else had she fallen for Gwen's crazy proposal about the shocking pink hat?

Philip Hannegan spoke up.

"I have reason to believe that Leland was killed by somebody entirely outside this family," he said. Gwen shook her head at him. "Inspector Bradish, may I speak with you privately? What I have to tell you is of a confidential nature, unless it does happen, as I think, to have some connection with Leland's death."

I caught Patrick's eye. His lips said "Coffee." I got it, and said at once, "Would anybody else besides me like coffee? If so, may I go make it, Inspector Bradish?"

The Inspector hesitated. Coffee would taste very good, he was thinking. He granted his permission. Patrick objected at once to my going alone to the kitchen. The Inspector ran his eye around the room. His own men were busy searching the house. Philip Hannegan had something urgent to tell him. The others were all suspects. Without further to-do, therefore, he gave Patrick permission to go to the kitchen with me.

"That was luck," Patrick said, as we got into the back hall. He went into the kitchen with me. "You put on plenty of coffee, with cold water. I'm going to look around." He returned in a couple of minutes. I had just got the coffee ready in the biggest coffeepot I could find and was turning on the gas when Patrick came back. "Turn it low so it won't boil over, and come along," he said.

He led the way through the passage into the garage under Mary Wong's apartment. We had left our raincoats in the living room and it was just as well, for our dark clothes blended with the darkness as we slipped out and made our way behind one of the hedges which hemmed the drive out to the street.

Luck favored us. As we got to the end of the hedge at the sidewalk we saw in the misty light of the street-lamp the police cars lined up in the rain, but up ahead, beside the vacant lot, stood our taxicab—the one Gwen had brought us and which had taken us to the police headquarters and then back here.

Patrick hustled me inside and asked the driver to take us to Powell and Broadway.

"Make it snappy," he said, after we were on the move. "I'm trying to put a fast one over on the police."

The driver was delighted. He was already hopping mad because a patrolman had pushed him around when he tried to get into the house to see what had happened to his fares. "And me only wanting my money!" he said, over his shoulder, as he clipped down the wet shiny hill and skidded at the turn into Pacific Street. He righted the car, expertly, and then said, "I didn't know who you was then, see. They tell me you're Patrick Abbott, the detective? Gosh!" He then said, "Lookey, there was something screwy about that dame. See? I picked her up over at a swell apartment house on Nob Hill and she tells me to drive her over to Russian Hill, and she gets out, along about where I was waiting for you, and then she sends me around to wait for her there at that place where you folks later on came out with her and got in the cab." That would have been in front of our apartment house. "She gets out in the wet and sends me away and after a while there's been this murder, see. I don't get it."

"How come her coat wasn't wet?" I said to Patrick.

Patrick let it go and said, to the driver, "I see what you mean."

"I ain't passing anything along to the police. If it's worth anything it's all yours, Pat."

The man's name and license number were mounted on the back of the front seat.

"Thanks. I appreciate that, Tony."

"You think I'm right about that dame, Pat?"

"Could be, Tony."

The driver then politely though reluctantly closed the window behind him to keep the cab dry.

I told Pat quickly about Gwen's proposal to Nancy about the hats.

"It requires a crazy system of lies, Pat. Gwen evidently thinks people are fools. She thinks if you keep saying a black thing's white that after a while, people will believe it."

"That's the advertising business," Patrick said.

"Don't joke, dear."

"I'm not joking. She's right."

"She's nuts, you mean. The awful thing is that Nancy apparently fell for it. Why? Oh, thank you for wanting me to come along, dear."

Patrick said, "I may need a stenographer, Jeanie."

"Oh." I felt rather flat.

Patrick put an arm around me and pulled me up close. "You're my girl! I couldn't run out on *you*. And, of course, I always need your opinions," he said then. "Go on about Gwen."

"Well, Gwen says Nancy isn't to answer any questions the police ask. Gwen's smart lawyer will fix what everybody is to say. They'll have to buy off a milliner here and a waiter here and there and this and that, but everything will be fine—so long as Nancy plays dumb. Gwen actually thinks Nancy is guilty, or seems to, and, honestly, if she didn't murder those two people why on earth would she agree to a cockeyed proposal like Gwen's? And why would Gwen make it?"

"Maybe Gwen hopes to hang on to the Leland advertising accounts," Patrick said.

"Sure. Also, Nancy is to lay off Philip Hannegan. Gwen said so. Gwen wants him herself. It's insane."

"White slavery up-to-date, huh?"

"Don't joke, darling. Did you see the look on Nancy's face when Phil came in? She loves him. And he loves her. Even policemen know about love. They'll use her feelings to make her talk. There's a goat, of course. Our client, Chris Leland, is to take the rap. I mean, our former client. Gwen's very helpful there. She will swear that he came out here purposely to kill his father and, and all."

We had been stopped by a red light.

Patrick said, "The police picked Chris up a short time ago, Jean. Headquarters phoned Bradish that they caught him trying to stuff a parcel into a mailbox. The parcel contained a .32-calibre automatic pistol. The box was a shoebox. In the box was the duplicate slip for a pair of shoes charged six days ago to a certain Mrs. Patrick Abbott."

"My goodness!" I caught my breath. "I left the bill in the box!"

"You always do, dear," Patrick said. "By the way, Helen Moore was shot with a .32-calibre automatic pistol."

"How do they know?"

"You must have seen me pick up the cartridge shell?" I remembered his swooping after something, folding it into his handkerchief. "I passed it along to Bradish. Meanwhile somebody gouged the bullet out of the plaster near the front door. There was a clean fingerprint on that shell. After the ballistics boys do their stuff on the gun, the bullet, and the shell maybe everything will be just fine. Maybe that will prove that Chris Leland killed Helen Moore. Then they will make him own up to murdering his father and Gwen will have been right all the time."

His voice sounded dry and bitter.

"But what about the pink hat?" I asked.

"Oh, yes," Patrick said vaguely. "That hat."

There wasn't time now to talk more about Gwen's schemes to explain the hat. "Look, Pat, Helen was shot from inside the house. That is, if they found the bullet in the entry."

"Bradish was having the house searched for the pistol when headquarters phoned that Chris had been picked up trying to get rid of the gun. He stopped the search. Now, Helen Moore had no key to the house. She must have slipped the catch on the front door when she went out. Chris could certainly have slipped in, waited for her, and shot her. Maybe he followed her from our place. We don't know when he left his room. He could have hidden in the halls, or outside. Maybe Chris saw Helen come to our place, maybe he went to Nancy's, got in through the unlocked door and waited for her. There wasn't any clip in his gun, or in his pockets, and not even a cartridge in the chamber, when I checked it. But maybe he had hidden his ammunition outside somewhere. Maybe he planned to get Helen. Maybe he thinks she knew he killed Leland. Maybe she went up on the hill with Leland last night. Maybe she witnessed his murder. We have only her word that she didn't, and that's no good now."

"She left Leland to catch a train."

Patrick said, "There is no one o'clock train to Los Angeles. She must have used a plane. Bradish checked them all, going and coming, last night. If anybody named Helen Moore had been a passenger on any flight, he would know it. But she must have flown home, under an assumed name."

"Do you think Chris did it, after all?"

Patrick said, pugnaciously, "I know darn well what I believe. But how the hell do I prove it?"

"How do they know Helen had no key?"

"From Rufus."

We were arriving near Powell and Broadway.

"Gwen has known Helen all their lives, Pat. She talked about her while you were in the morgue. She implied things, mostly about Helen's fine clothes. She said Helen said her mother paid for her clothes, and that she moved to San Diego because Helen was ashamed of her—you heard that part . . ."

Patrick groaned. "If only I had time! I know a good operative in San Diego—there are things I need to know about Helen's background—but I—well, first I'm going to play the hunch that brought me down here."

We got out. Patrick told Tony where we were going but asked him to drive ahead around the corner, and wait for us along the block. "If we don't show up in half an hour call up Inspector Bradish at that house we just left, Tony."

Tony jotted Nancy Leland's telephone number and slipped it in his cap-band. He moved on, and we walked back a short distance. Now, Patrick said, as we came to that Mexican dive, we were going to take things up where we shouldn't have left off in the first place, had we known how to look into the future. We entered. We were not welcomed. The man who seemed to be the headwaiter or a captain hurried toward us, frowning. It was too late to serve liquors, he said. Patrick said we'd have cokes. But the orchestra was just about to stop for the night, he said. The customers were at the point of leaving. As we could see, he said, his tone full of petulance, not many remained here now. Patrick took out his card, handed it to the man, told him to hand that to the manager of the place, and guided me around the man and toward the table we'd had last night. It was unoccupied. At the next table—the big one with the banquette where Ernest Leland and Helen Moore had sat last night—half a dozen kids were again drinking those Purple Passions—grape juice spiked with vodka, or rum, or what-have-you. They were squealing and giggling.

The waiter was a different one from last night's. "Where's the regular man?" Patrick asked. "Let's see—was his name Pedro?"

The man's jet eyes went blank. He hunched up his shoulders. "Marco," he said. "I don't know where he is."

"Friend of yours?" Patrick asked.

The man gave a quick shake of his head.

"Okay, bring us two cokes," Patrick said. "Step on it, please. We're in a hurry."

The man caught a glance from the captain, and hurried. Quite a contrast to the sleepy waiter we had had last night. I glanced about the room. The kids at the table where Ernest Leland and Helen Moore had sat were very hilarious.

The captain returned, walking with a triumphant little twist. "Sorry. Mr. Legendre can't see you tonight. He says come back tomorrow sometime, better in the afternoon."

Patrick said, "Legendre? And you call this place Mexican?"

The man shrugged. "Mr. Legendre is sorry he cannot see you, Mr. Abbott."

Patrick spoke slowly. "I wonder what police headquarters will do to this joint when I tell them you're giving kids goof-balls?"

The man looked scared. "That's not so!" he said.

Patrick said, "I'm not unknown at headquarters. They'll take my word. The kids at the next table are drinking vodka, which you've probably sold them after hours. They're getting a cheap jag by swallowing barbiturate tablets with the vodka. They were doing it last night when we were here. What's more, they all look under twenty-one, which means they've no business even to be here." The man had started to fidget. "Will Legendre come out here or do I go to his office to see him?" Patrick said.

"I'll ask him again, sir," the waiter said politely. "You being served all right?"

"Perfectly. But I miss Marco," Patrick said.

The man stiffened, and hurried away. The new waiter brought the cokes and glowed when Patrick gave him a good tip. The imitation-Mexican orchestra stopped its Harry-James-imitation and started wearily putting away its instruments.

In a very short time Mr. Legendre came to our table. He was a bald man, with oyster-white eyes, gray lips, and a wolfish set of yellow teeth. He was affable. He offered a puffy clammy hand and said to come into his office, that there was no law against a man giving a friend a friendly drink of Scotch at any time of night. Patrick declined.

"We're in a hurry," he said. He waved a hand at me. "My secretary will take down anything you can tell us about your waiter Marco, Mr. Legendre. First, his full name and his home address."

I took a small note pad and pencil from my handbag.

Mr. Legendre squirmed. "I don't know his full name and address," he said. "Why do you ask?" He turned suddenly on the captain. "Get those kids at the next table out of here. Fast!" he said. "Look, Mr. Abbott," he said, sitting down now, and offering a cigar, which he returned to his pocket after Patrick declined it, "we don't sell those pills to our customers. We don't know where they get them, and, unless we catch them using the stuff..."

"That oughtn't to be hard. If your waiters have any eyes."

"I know," Mr. Legendre said. "But the war—the labor shortage—everything—you can't do everything, Mr. Abbott."

Patrick cut in. "Well, about Marco..."

"I don't know anything about Marco..."

"Take down everything," Patrick said to me, interrupting Legendre. "Your social security's all in order, I suppose? In that case you'll have most of the information I'll need about this man."

Legendre looked sick. He rallied, and answered promptly thereafter. He didn't know anything about Marco except that he was a good waiter. He had him listed as Jones, but had suspected that wasn't his right name. Sometimes he didn't show up for a couple of days, otherwise he was a good enough waiter. Good as you'd get. He'd been here ever since the place opened up, a year and a half ago now. He lived on Stockton Street, not far from here, but Mr. Legendre had never been to his place. He managed to remember the number. It was a hotel, he thought. Marco was not, to his knowledge, married. Why was the inquiry being made? Had something happened?

Patrick got up abruptly, ending the interview. We had not touched our drinks. We left the place with Mr. Legendre running after us, his gray lips imploring us to stay a little longer, to let him have a chance to show some hospitality.

The cab waited. Patrick gave the address on Stockton Street. "I know that dump," Tony said. "It's no good, Pat."

"You wait outside, Tony. And call Bradish if we don't come out in ten minutes or so."

"That's no place for a lady to go into," Tony said.

"The lady is my wife and my assistant," Patrick said.

"Well, be careful," Tony said, as he drew up and we got out to go into the hotel.

It had a funny smell. The hotel was on the second floor and the smell began the minute you came off the street and started climbing the old worn-out stairs. There was a tiny cubicle of an office. Inside, an old dried-up man slept on a filthy cot just under the wicket.

"I don't know where Marco is," he whined, when Patrick roused him. "He ain't been home since last night. First time he ever stayed away. Nice feller. Always pays his rent right on the dot."

"I want to see his room," Patrick said.

"You from the police?"

"Missing persons bureau," Patrick lied.

The old man got up and got some keys. He gave off a concentrated dose of the odor we'd met in the stairs. It was a mixture of filth and something else.

Marco Jones's room, on the second floor at the end of the hall, overlooking the street, was permeated with that fetid evil smell. Its illumination was a single droplight. Old lace curtains, grim from caked grime, covered its two windows. A birdcage hung in one window. It was covered, and the bird began to chirp plaintively as soon as we came in. While Patrick went over the room in his quick painstaking way the old man hung about in the door. I took the cover off the cage and got the bird some water from the pitcher that stood on an old-fashioned washstand. There was some birdseed behind the pitcher, so I fed the bird. Its cage contributed somewhat to the foul smell of the room.

Patrick went about, tapping walls, looking under the dirty rug, examining the contents of drawers and the shallow closet, and so on.

He asked the old man, "Every so often I wouldn't be surprised if Marco hung a wet blanket over the door and stayed home a couple of days, didn't he?"

The creepy eyes slithered. "I don't know nothing about anything like that."

"You can smell, can't you?"

"I never noticed anything out of the way. Marco always paid his rent regular."

"Anybody ever come to visit him?"

"Not to stay," the old man said. "He always behaved all right. He's a good roomer."

"You'd remember any people who came?"

"Can't say that I could."

Patrick said, "The police may help you remember."

The man wavered, and after a moment said, "There wasn't many. I guess maybe—if I was sure of protection—but even so, I don't know any names or where anybody lives. I never ask any questions so I'm never told any lies, see."

"Did a tall distinguished-looking man with gray hair on the temples ever come here?" Patrick asked. The old man shook his head. "Or a golden-haired woman with fine clothes?"

"Nobody like that. Old, hard-up people, was the only kind that ever came to see Marco." The man cackled. "Old like me. Before their time."

Back outside the drizzle seemed by contrast very fresh and lovely. "Now where?" Tony asked, eagerly.

"Home," Patrick said.

Tony looked disappointed as he headed again toward Russian Hill.

I said to Patrick, "Just what is this all about, Pat?"

"Marco's the man in the morgue," Patrick said. "He was picked up dead on the street. He was identified by a fake social security card as Miguel Nogales. His address was a place in Los Angeles. Why did Marco die so soon after Leland?"

"Why should there be any connection?"

"Maybe there isn't," Patrick said.

"By the way, what was that funny smell in that hotel?"

"Opium," Patrick said.

FIFTEEN

Two dimmed lamps glowed sedately in the dignified lobby just inside the front door. Two more burned beside the Spanish-style ironwork of the elevator. Vincent Smith slept, stretched out with room to spare on the garnet velvet cushions of a Spanish-style couch. We let him sleep. We slipped past softly, and tiptoed up the five flights to our apartment.

I felt bushed. All the horror, suspense, suspicion, the worry, the conflict of personalities, the violent passions, the physical discomfort from my damp clothing, the fatigue—all seemed to gang up on me as we reached home. I said, as Patrick shut the door, and then headed along the lighted hall to the kitchen, "Thank God, we can call it a day."

He made no answer. He flicked the light switch. The kitchen appeared in all its white brilliance.

"What are you going to do now?"

He answered brusquely.

"Call John Grace in San Diego."

"Who's he?"

"The operative I told you about. I want a check-up on Helen Moore's mother. I want to find out just how ill she is. And also anything else. I got her full name and address from Rufus Moore tonight—while Bradish wasn't listening, I hope."

I was standing in the kitchen door when he picked up the phone which was plugged in beside the dinette table.

"Fix us a drink," Patrick said. He sounded short.

I got cross. It was unreasonable, but there you are.

"We don't need a drink," I said. "We need to go to bed."

"Huh-uh," Patrick said. He gave the operator Grace's full name and his address in San Diego.

"You know darn well that can wait till morning," I said. I just went on standing in the door. "Pat, you're a fool. Why do you bother? What do you get out of it? Nothing but a lot of work and worry and a headache all the way round."

The operator asked for our number and said she would call back. Patrick cradled the receiver, then took out his cigarette papers and his little sack of tobacco. He said, "If the cigarette shortage keeps on I've got to get one of those waterproof tobacco sacks they use in England."

I said, getting mad again, "If you weren't so darned slow you'd have cigarettes. Does Gwen Telfer have to roll her own? Or Philip Hannegan? Or Rufus Moore or Sam Bradish?"

"We don't know what they do in secret."

"That is not funny!"

"And me thinking it quite good, Jeanie."

"I don't think it's any time for cracks, Pat."

Patrick peeled off a paper and shook the tobacco onto it. The paper stayed steady as a rock. He manipulated the strings of the sack with two fingers and dropped it back into his pocket. He was still in his raincoat and hat. He rolled the cigarette, offered it to me, and when I shook my head, calmly put it between his lips and lit it. His keen blue eyes stayed steady on the flame until he blew it out and tossed the match into an ashtray on the table.

It made me furious. Here I was, absolutely dead, absolutely in a complete tizzy over all the goings-on, and there he was, calm as you please. Taking his own sweet time. I said things. I said plenty about what I thought of people who let other people give them the run-around.

"I'm going to have a bath and go to bed," I said finally.

If he had tried to keep me, I would have stayed.

But he said nothing. He crossed to the cupboard where we kept what liquor we had and took down our one bottle of Scotch.

"Sure you wouldn't like one, dear?"

"I told you that I'm taking a bath and going to bed."

"Sorry. Hate to drink alone," Patrick said. But he went right ahead doing it.

I started to the bedroom to get ready for my bath.

It wasn't too late yet. I could turn back. I could still ask why he thought the death of a waiter called Marco was so important that he had sneaked away to that dive just at a time when the police would be closing in on Nancy Leland.

I stopped.

The telephone rang.

"Fast work!" Patrick said. He set down the glass and took the call.

I waited in the hall, slowly divesting myself of my raincoat.

"Hello? Why, hello, Sam! Well, it was like this. I got afraid if we stuck around any longer you'd keep us there all night. You knew where to find me, didn't you? Is that so? Well, I told you there before I left that

I thought your experts would find that that bullet was *not* fired by Chris Leland's gun. No, I'm not God, Sam. If I were a lot of things wouldn't happen. I just use my head. You're sure that the house has been thoroughly searched for the right gun? Um-m . . . Now, look here, Sam, you lay off me for an hour or so and I'll bring you home the bacon. . . . I know it looks funny, but . . . Give me an hour then and . . . oh, don't be a damn fool, Sam . . . You've got them all there right in the house. All you have to do is watch them. Sooner or later the guilty one is bound to crack. . . . Oh, you know who did it? That's fine!" Patrick's voice struck a sarcastic note.

I stood listening.

"Thanks, Sam. . . . I'll be here if you want me . . . Any time . . . By the way, there's a fellow named Legendre who runs a dive off Powell Street. If I were you I'd pick him up for questioning about that guy you've got in the morgue. The one you've labeled Nogales." Bradish must have asked why. "I say his murder hooks up in some way with that of Ernest Leland. . . . I didn't say they were both killed by the same party, Sam."

Patrick put down the receiver after a moment and picked up his Scotch.

I said, "Anything new?"

"Yes. The bullet they dug out of the wall in the entrance hall wasn't fired by Chris Leland's pistol. But the cartridge shell I picked up beside the body had one of Chris's fingerprints on it, all the same."

"Meaning?"

"Meaning the shot was fired from another gun. Why not? Chris said that somebody snitched his ammunition. Answer: Find out which suspect owns a .32-calibre automatic Colt pistol. Lots of them in the world. Popular size and style. Sam was mad because I picked up the shell, even though by doing it I saved its being fingered by some patrolman or somebody. I think he thinks I also snitched the murder gun."

I said, "Of all the utter confusion . . ."

"It's as simple as the nose on your face."

"Don't show off," I said.

The telephone rang one long hard ring.

Patrick grabbed it. In a moment he was giving instructions to John Grace in San Diego. He told Grace he had to have a lot of information and right now. No, tomorrow morning wouldn't do. Too much was at stake. In a few hours too much trouble could happen. People could get away. Yes, the sooner the better. Under cover, of course. Patrick gave Grace this phone number. He said if he got no answer here to call Nancy Leland. He carefully gave her address and telephone number.

He hung up. He again picked up his drink and began to walk up and down the kitchen.

"Are we going over there again, Pat?"

"Of course."

"Well, I'm not going. If you want those notes I took in that dive they're in my bag."

"I don't want them," Patrick said. "I just wanted us to look official."

"Oh, go to hell!" I said, mad all over again.

There is almost nothing a bath can't fix, at least a little. I know that. I kept my mind on it firmly while I went on into the bedroom. I snapped on the lights and laid my handbag on the table. There it had lain earlier tonight. There Chris had opened it, stealing the stamps, and maybe some small change. From that closet he had taken the shoebox. We would have to explain that, too.

I felt all in. I felt almost ill with anxiety as I stripped off my jacket, dropped my skirt, pulled my sweater over my head and unhooked my bra. But the Scot in me—that MacGregor streak on my mother's side—reminded me even in a moment like this to go easy with my girdle, one of only two left of the pre-war model I had long preferred.

I left everything on a chair, except the girdle which I put away on a shelf in the closet. I put on my terry robe and thrust my feet into a pair of terrycloth scuffs.

The telephone rang. Patrick took it in the kitchen. I slipped over to the open door and listened.

"Yes, Sam . . . I have to wait here, Sam. I'm waiting for a long-distance call, see . . . Yeah, I know I can have it put through to me over there, but—my wife's taking a bath. Nope, I don't want to leave her here alone . . . Yes, I think I know where the gun is, but . . . Look here, Sam, keep your shirt on. The minute I can come over I'll come, and if my hunch about that gun isn't right I'll eat it—the gun, not the hunch, Samuel. . . . Okay, Inspector Bradish. You can count on me, but my wife gets her bath first, see. Yeah, I know it's a funny time to take a bath but it's her bath, Sam. Everything she does is all right by me."

I felt better immediately. I went back to the bathroom, dropped my robe and slippers, and stepped into the shower.

The water came too hot at first. I got mad all over again. Then I got the taps adjusted and the water surged down just the right temperature. It knocked out all the kinks. Right away my brain started to function and my temper improved.

After a while I made the water a little cooler. Patrick would not mind if I stretched out my bath. He had to wait for John Grace, too. He wouldn't mind my taking my time.

I was shivering. The water was running stone cold. I shut it off and stepped out on the bath-mat. I started rubbing myself dry. I went into the bedroom and got out clean clothes. All was silence in the kitchen. I dressed, taking my time. Clean and dry from the skin out to a fresh brown tweed suit. I went back into the bath to put on my make-up.

Somewhere a door closed, softly. I listened. The sound had come from the kitchen. Patrick closing the service door, I supposed. Checking up. We had left the lock off when we went out, remember, in case Chris should return.

The telephone started ringing.

I gave my hair a couple of pats and hurried along to get in on the talk. I stepped into the hall.

The kitchen lights had been switched off. The phone was ringing in darkness.

A door had closed, too softly. The telephone rang and nobody answered.

It stopped ringing. The air was cruelly empty of all sound.

"Pat?" I called. I made my voice low.

There was no answer.

The phone started to ring again. I waited. The darkness seemed crawling with danger. I stood in an agony of fear trying to decide what to do.

SIXTEEN

The elevator cage stopped on our floor. Standing in the dark I heard the door of the cage slide back, then the grill. Neither closed. But only one set of footsteps crossed the tiles to our door. Vincent Smith, I thought, with a fresh shiver, as our door-bell rang.

It was at least someone, however, and I came alive and ran to answer, snapping on the hall lights on my way.

Mary Wong, in her old black coat, was outside. Vincent Smith was in the elevator door, waiting, with his weasel eyes gleaming, to see what she wanted.

The very sight of that man put me on the alert. I invited Mary in and closed the door. We moved from the entry into the main hall of the apartment.

Eight inches taller than Mary, I looked down on her and told her how frightened I was and how Patrick had mysteriously disappeared. "The telephone keeps ringing. I'm afraid to go out there to answer it. Perhaps he came over to your house?" I said.

"That is possible," Mary Wong said, in her flat voice. "The house is not well guarded. There is only one man outside, and he stays by the front door. I slipped out through the garage and the vacant lot. I am here to ask Mr. Patrick please to come to our house. They are worrying Miss Nancy."

"Who is?" I asked.

"Those policemen."

"Did Nancy send you?"

She nodded. "I could slip away because my rooms are away from the house," she said. "But I must hurry."

The telephone started ringing again, its bell loud in its box here in the hall.

"Now that you're here I'm not afraid to answer," I said.

A long groan sounded in the kitchen.

I ran, with Mary Wong trotting at my heels. I snapped on the lights.

Patrick lay, with blood all around him, on the linoleum beside the dinette table. Above him the telephone kept up its futile ringing.

I dropped down beside Patrick. He opened an eye and growled thickly, "Answer that phone. It drives me crazy." He tried to sit up. "Oops," he said, and lay down again. "Darling . . ." I said. I began to cry.

"I'm all right. It's only a nosebleed. *Answer that phone, for God's sake!*"

"I will make compresses," Mary Wong said. Patrick opened the eye and looked at her. "Hello," he said, with an attempt at a smile.

I answered the phone.

Bradish said, "Where the hell have you all been?" Then he said, politely, "Excuse me, is this Mrs. Abbott? I've been trying to call you for ten minutes."

I said, with rare presence of mind, for me, "The operator must have rung the wrong number."

Bradish grunted.

"Is Pat there, Mrs. Abbott?" he asked, with politeness now.

I slanted an eye at my prostrate spouse.

"I can call him—if it's urgent."

"Just tell him to come on over. Pronto. You come too, Mrs. Abbott."

"All right," I said. "It's Bradish," I said, cradling the thing. "He wants us to come right over."

Mary Wong was already bathing Patrick's face, with quick deft movements. "That feels good, Mary," he said. "I'm all right. I'm not jumping right up though, because I don't want to be sick. We'll have to go, Jeanie."

"Mary came for us, dear," I said.

"Did Bradish send you, Mary?"

The Chinese woman shook her head. "I was allowed to go to my room and lie down after the police got finished asking me very many questions. As I walked out of the living room the Inspector followed me and asked the policeman who was watching the kitchen if he would call up police headquarters and have them bring the hat. There was a hat found in Mr. Leland's car which the Inspector says was Miss Nancy's. I know for certain that Miss Nancy never once wore the hat. I think it will help her very much for me to say this, but it is better if you are there to help us, I think."

"That's right, Mary. Jean, will you get me another coat? Anything will do. This one looks like a butcher's."

"Don't talk and worry yourself," I said.

"Would you swear she never wore the hat?" Patrick was asking as I went out. "Would you hold up your hand and say so, before witnesses?"

Mary Wong seemed puzzled at first, then her face lit up and she said, "Yes, of course."

I got an overcoat for Patrick.

Something was certainly haywire. I had heard that door close while I was dressing. But Patrick must have taken the fall *while I was still in the shower.* With the water pelting I couldn't've heard thunder itself. So the door had been closed after he was unconscious.

Who had closed the door?

Chris had gone out and left that door unlocked.

How many people knew that?

Helen Moore had known it. Helen had turned the knob and found it open. But Helen was dead. Had she been observed coming in? Had she talked with anyone on her way to Nancy's?

Vincent Smith, the elevator man, probably knew the door was unlocked. He might have sneaked around and discovered it.

Gwen Telfer might know from Vincent Smith that the door was not locked.

Gwen had talked with Vincent down in the lobby before we got down. How politely—and how unlike him—he had opened the door when we left the house in Gwen's company! Money talks when handed to people like Vincent Smith. You can kill by deputy. No other method would interest Gwendolyn Telfer.

My dislike and suspicion of Gwen Telfer had taken a bitter active turn as I returned to the kitchen.

Patrick was sitting on a chair now, and blowing his nose. Mary Wong was mopping up the blood from the linoleum. She did the job neatly, and with an efficiency which would have satisfied even Gwendolyn Telfer. She first blotted the blood up with paper towels. She sleuthed out a mop from the broom closet.

Patrick made himself a cigarette.

"How do I look, Jeanie?"

"Awful," I said. "Your nose is getting roundish. I think you will have a black eye. But at least you didn't get shot and you aren't dead from cyanide."

He tried to grin, but his face hurt.

"Don't be silly, Jean. I took my own header. You know how the insurance people are always telling you that the greatest hazards are right in your own home. This waxed floor, for instance . . ."

"Oh, Pat."

"What happened to the coffee?" Patrick asked Mary Wong.

She smiled and said it had got finished and served.

Patrick lit the cigarette. Mary rinsed the spot with clear water. She didn't like the way the mop dried it. She found a clean rag and did the job right.

"I had to wait for that call," Patrick said, "so I decided to pour myself another drink and sit down and be comfortable. I poured the drink. Hand it to me, please, Mary." Mary got it, from beside the bottle on the sink. She finished drying the linoleum then, and carefully hung up the cloth out of sight on the rack in the broom closet, just as I would have done. "Then I pulled a boner," Patrick said. "I decided to snap off the lights, then pick up my drink, and turn on the table lamp after I sat down. You had already turned off the hall lights. The place went pitch dark. I slipped on the wax and cracked my head, hit it on the table." He grinned. "There's a bright side to this picture. At least I slipped before I picked up this Scotch." He downed the Scotch and stood up. "Let's go," he said.

Mary said, "Isn't it better if I slip back the way I came, Mr. Patrick? There is a gate from this back yard leading into Mr. Hannegan's garden, which is how I came in." I stared at her, thinking suddenly that Helen Moore probably used the same route. They all knew this hill better than we did. "Then I went around and came in the front way," Mary explained. "I was only trying to avoid the police at our house. But perhaps it is best if I return the same way? Then I will not be seen going back into the house. They would ask many questions. They would guess that Miss Nancy sent me here, perhaps."

"You've got something there, Mary. Okay. Come down with us, and then go back the other way. How did you get out of your house?"

"Through the garage." It was the way we had come out. "I can get back in the same way."

"All right. We'll keep the policeman at the front door busy while you get back into your place. Turn on a light when you get in. Is Rosalie with you tonight?"

"No," Mary said, thankfully. "If no lights come on it will mean they will have found the garage door unlocked, and if you could go in and lock it . . ."

"I'll do that."

After we left the kitchen I heard Patrick step over and lock the back door.

My heart pounded. So he knew that somebody had slipped into our kitchen? He had not slipped on the wax. He had been attacked. He knew everything, then. He had waited till he thought I was out of the room to lock that door, so that I would not notice. Or was he thinking of Mary Wong instead?

I watched Vincent Smith while he took the cage down. That slippery customer did not bother to bow us out this time. He stood eyeing us till we were near the front door, then he headed drowsily back to his garnet-velvet couch.

At the foot of the tiled steps from the portico Mary ducked through the driveway to the back and we walked along Green Street.

It was still raining. But the fog had lifted. The air smelled very fresh, and like the open ocean. The street lamps were beginning to sparkle a little and that foghorn on the prison island had stopped its mournful chanting.

Patrick sniffed the fine air. "Ouch!" he said then.

"Does your face hurt?"

"And how!"

"Darling, what really happened?"

He chuckled and pulled my arm close. "I got careless," he said. "I had that door on my mind all the time, but I was thinking about something else, and I neglected it."

"Somebody came in by that door?"

"Yep. And he bashed me in the back of the head. I hit my face on a table. He left me in the dark. But why didn't he finish the job? But maybe he thought he did."

"You're sure it was somebody?"

Patrick said, "Positive. I asked for it. I was careless."

"I blame myself. I heard the door close. I was out of the bath by that time. I thought you were seeing if the door was locked. I thought—I thought for a minute that you were walking out on me, but when I saw the lights were off I knew that was cockeyed. You might take a powder on me, Pat, but you wouldn't leave me in the dark. I took my own sweet time. It wasn't till the telephone kept ringing and ringing that I got scared. And there you were, lying in that blood."

"The detective business is too hard on a girl," Patrick said, soberly.

The Leland house stood dark in the rain. The police cars, except the Inspector's Buick, had gone away. Under the lamps burning beside the front entrance a solitary policeman in a shining raincoat kept his vigil.

We paused beside him. He knew Patrick, so it was not hard to divert him into giving his own opinions on the two murders, until Mary Wong's light appeared in the front windows of the room above the garage. We went into the house.

All the hall lights were on. There was a chalk line around the spot where Helen Moore had lain, and the great black stain from her blood.

We skirted the spot painstakingly.

We heard voices coming from the open door of the living room. We walked along the hall and entered. With a curt nod Bradish acknowledged us from his chair near this end of the two sofas. His stenographer sat on his left, behind a small table. Nancy Leland and Gwendolyn Telfer now faced each other from the two sofas. The fire burned well.

Between Nancy and Gwen, on a coffee table, resting on some tissue paper, was a pink feather hat.

Shocking-pink. Rose-color. It made a brilliant spot in the subdued greens and golds of this room.

Patrick sat down beside Nancy, I beside Gwen.

"Don't be stupid, Inspector!" Gwen was saying as we sat down.

Bradish winced.

"I'm not being stupid, Miss Telfer. I'm an overworked man. In our department every man nowadays does the work of two. I try to be patient, however. I have the milliner's word for the hat. This hat was bought ten days ago in her shop. It was a special order, so she isn't likely to forget about it. You went with Mrs. Leland to order the hat, but the hat was delivered to Mrs. Leland at this address."

"Fiddledeedee!" Gwen said airily. She was smoking, and she took time to inhale. "Nobody says Madeleine didn't make this hat. The trouble is that you're mixed up on the hats. There were two hats. One is pink and the other is blue. And they were both made for me. Madame Madeleine is acquainted with Mrs. Leland. For some reason the blue hat—which is the one she made ten days ago—was delivered here instead of to me. Afterwards Mrs. Leland herself fetched it along to me."

"And how did the red hat get into Leland's car?"

"Pink," Gwen corrected him. "Shocking-pink. I left it there myself!"

"Very interesting, Miss Telfer. Then you were in Leland's car just before it crashed down this hill?"

"Don't be silly! I dined with Ernest Leland two evenings before he left for Mexico. I didn't see him after he returned. That night I was wearing the pink hat. I must have left it in his car."

"You can prove that?"

Gwen said slowly, "I can't prove that I left it in his car. But it is self-evident. I thought I had lost the hat. I didn't know where the hat was, you see. Had I known it was in his car I should have collected the darn thing from his garage, instead of forking out forty-five bucks for almost a duplicate . . ."

"Forty-five dollars?" Bradish gasped.

"Forty-five, ninety-five, to be exact. There is no ceiling on French hats, Inspector Bradish."

"Forty-five bucks!" Bradish gasped. "No wonder they call it shocking. And I don't refer to the color, Miss Telfer."

Gwen ignored it. "Madeleine makes oceans of hats," she prattled. "She is probably confused about this one. If you will call her again I am sure she will make everything clear."

Bradish watched her.

"There was a hair in the hat, Miss Telfer," he said, succinctly.

With her thumb Gwen flipped her cigarette, but half smoked, at the fireplace.

"Perfectly normal place to find a hair, Inspector."

"It's a black hair, Miss Telfer. Your hair is—ah . . ."

"Taffy-colored," Gwen laughed. Her eyes, laughing, held the Inspector's sparkling gaze. "Red. Sandy. What you will. Well, why not a black hair in the hat? Maybe it was tried on in the shop? Maybe one of your policemen tried it on, when your back was turned . . ."

Bradish smiled foxily.

"So far as I am aware, Miss Telfer, no member of the force has lately had a permanent wave . . ."

Gwen pounced. "What do you mean permanent wave?"

Bradish moved his hunched shoulders.

"What is usually meant, Miss Telfer. There was a hair in the hat. It had been permanently waved. Indeed, in the laboratory they will be able to tell you in due time when it was waved, and by what process, and even, approximately, who did it . . ."

Gwen cut in triumphantly. "I am not questioning the expert research done by your wonder boys, Inspector Bradish. But you missed the bus. Mrs. Leland's hair has a natural wave. She has never had it permed in her life."

Nancy Leland watched Gwen with astonishment and real admiration. Bradish shifted his gaze to Patrick, who certainly was nothing much to look at just now, with his face out of shape.

"What happened to you, Pat?" he asked. Anything to get away from Gwennie, I thought.

"I tangled with a table," Patrick said. "And I was thinking, while you were talking, that I had never seen Nancy Leland wear that color, Sam."

Again we looked at the hat.

SEVENTEEN

Inspector Bradish whirled on Patrick.

He evidently counted ten, then said, "I'll talk to you later. Privately."

"The sooner the better, Sam," Patrick said.

Bradish ignored him.

"Now, all of you! You're staying in this house till I break this case, see? There's lots of police business much more important than yours. I don't suppose you believe that? I don't suppose," he repeated, his glance focusing on Gwendolyn Telfer, "that you can even imagine anything in this world can be as important as yourselves? Hah!" He turned to the stenographer, a callow young fellow with large red ears. "Go upstairs and tell Inspector Cook to bring those guys back here. Pronto."

"Yes, sir," said the boy. He pussyfooted out of the room. There are people whose attempts to be quiet are noisier than average human behavior, and he was one. He knocked his chair over. Near the door he brushed Inspector Bradish's raincoat off another chair. It hit the carpet with the dullish thud that suggests, in the pocket of a policeman, nothing in this world save a gun. He cast back an anguished glance, picked up the coat and put it where it had been, and left the room. His clumsiness, on top of all the rest, made Bradish quite speechless from rage.

There were sounds of arrival in the front hall. A police sergeant came in with Chris Leland.

Chris was dirty, had a black eye, a piece of skin was off his freckled small nose, and he looked worried.

He met Patrick's grin with a baffled gaze which changed into a steady, set look.

"Glad to see you're all in one piece," Patrick said.

Chris licked his upper lip. "You don't look so hot yourself," he mumbled.

"Tangled with a table, Chris." Patrick's sorry smile must have got across because the kid smiled back.

"It wasn't a table in my case, Mr. Abbott."

"I'm running this show," Bradish said. "Now suppose you sit down and tell us how you happen to be so well acquainted with *Mister* Abbott, Chris."

The boy was then put on a straight chair which the police sergeant pulled up facing Bradish. The detective tilted a lampshade so that bright light shone full on his battered face. Chris did not answer the Inspector's question.

The two girls watched young Chris. Gwen Telfer's turquoise eyes were gleaming hard as agates. Frank curiosity animated Nancy's long dark eyes.

Chris sat squinting under the bright light.

Bradish took another tack, and asked, civilly, "I think you know everybody here, don't you, Chris?"

"He doesn't know me," Nancy said. She jumped up and shook hands with the boy and told him her name. Her transforming smile changed her completely, as always. Bradish eyed them suspiciously, as though he thought they were putting on an act.

"Sit down, Mrs. Leland," he said, but patiently. "Now, Chris, I want to know just how you fit into this picture, please." Chris did not reply. He was watching Nancy. How come this beautiful gal married a louse like my father? his eyes were saying. Bradish lifted his voice. "I want you to explain, Chris, how it happens that a woman was murdered tonight with a bullet from a shell which has one of your fingerprints on it? Wait a minute," he stopped himself. "Do you know shorthand, Mrs. Abbott? If so, will you substitute temporarily as my stenographer?" I nodded. "Thank you."

I moved from the sofa to the little table. The steno's notebook lay open. We used the same method. My eye was caught by a notation set down before we came in. It was, "Inspector Bradish: Okay. If Pat Abbott's mixed up with this horrible crime he'll find I'm no respecter of special persons."

Oh, dear. My hand quivered as I held the pencil ready to take the notes.

"Answer," Bradish said to Chris.

"Well," Chris said, "I'll admit I broke into somebody's bag and stole some stamps. I'm sorry. I was going to explain it as soon as I saw them."

"You mean Mrs. Abbott's bag, don't you, Chris?" The boy did not reply. "How come you went to the Abbott apartment?" Chris dropped his long-lashed eyelids, perhaps because of the electric glare from the light. He said nothing. "Don't take all day, Chris." No answer. "Why, then, did you try to get rid of the gun?"

Chris replied, "I couldn't stand to have the thing around another minute. It was driving me nuts. It wasn't my gun. I decided it might make me a lot of trouble, so I tried to send it back to its owner."

Inspector Bradish snorted.

"You knew that once in the mails we couldn't lay hands on it till it reached its destination. You knew it would take a week or ten days the way the mails are now before it arrived. You needed that time, or thought you did."

"No, I just wanted to get rid of it," said Chris.

Bradish said, "Look here, Chris. Don't stall. We know you went to the Abbotts'. We've got that shoebox and we know where you got it. We have a man who saw you go there, too."

Patrick said, "Sure, he came there. He was scared and hungry. We fed him and put him to bed. Too bad he didn't stay put."

Bradish said, largely, "Well, well. And what made you go to Pat Abbott, Chris?"

"Well—well, I read in the papers that the police were after me. I thought I needed some advice."

"But why Pat Abbott?"

"He is a famous detective," said Chris.

Bradish laughed.

"Hear, hear! 'Way back East in Connecticut, clear across the great American continent, they know about Patrick Abbott. Do tell!"

Chris said miserably, "A man told me to go to Mr. Abbott."

"What man?"

"A man in—a man in a park," Chris lied. He flushed, too.

All at once Inspector Bradish dropped the sarcastic tone and went on in a reasonable tone.

"See here, Chris. You're just a kid. There is no sense in your taking the rap for somebody who is old enough to know better. Who sent you to Abbott?"

The kid sat in silence.

Bradish went on as if monologuing. "Nancy Leland owns a pistol. She admitted it, though unwillingly, just before you came in." I shot a look at Nancy and saw her face go pale and her teeth sink worriedly into her underlip. "It's a .32-calibre automatic Colt pistol exactly like the one you tried to get rid of, Chris. She says she had no ammunition. *You gave her yours*. She told you that when your father was dead you two would split his dough fifty-fifty. You wanted him dead. So she used you. It was her idea, see. You'll get clemency, Chris. You tell us the truth and we'll see that you get a fair deal. You're young. No use your dying in the gas chamber for something a grown-up woman dreamed up. . . . *Mrs. Abbott, you are not taking notes!*"

"I'm sorry," I said. "It's just too silly to be set down."

"That's for me to decide, Mrs. Abbott."

"I'm sorry."

I held the pencil ready.

"Well, it is silly," Chris said. "I never even saw Nancy Leland till tonight. She never had a chance to borrow my bullets, or talk to me even. Besides, the papers say my father died from cyanide poisoning."

That I wrote down.

Bradish said sarcastically—and I put down the word sarcastic in parentheses after the question, "Is that so? You never even heard of her, I suppose?"

"Sure, I heard of her. My aunt said he had married a young girl. She knew her name was Nancy. I don't know how my aunt knew, though. In the phone book I found her as Mrs. Ernest K. Leland."

"When?"

"Night before last."

"What did you do then?"

"I called up. Nobody answered, so I came over here. But I never saw her. She wasn't home, I guess."

"So you left the clip from your gun, stuffed with cartridges, for her to use at her leisure," said Bradish.

"Why, no. Why should I?"

"Okay. Okay. What did you do then?"

"I went back to the hotel where Mr. Hannegan had got me a room."

Bradish almost danced with excitement.

"*Hannegan* got you a room?"

Chris fidgeted. "Well, he helped me. He knew the manager of the hotel, or I guess maybe I wouldn't've got it. Rooms are very hard to find here."

Bradish grinned hard. "I see. Nancy Leland's boy friend got you the room. What else did he do to help you, Chris? Told you to call up Nancy, didn't he? Or to come and see her here?"

"Now, you see here, Mr. Bradish," Chris said, stubbornly. "Mr. Hannegan is a nice guy. He got me the room because he said if I would go to bed and get some rest I'd forget what—what I came out here to do. He's a hundred per cent. He took my gun and put it in his desk and if I had left it there it would be a lot better for everybody . . ."

"What's that, Chris?" Bradish cried excitedly. "He took your gun? Holy cow! Maybe I'm putting the horse before the cart. Now we're cooking with gas. Hannegan slipped out the clip, then, and passed it along to his girl friend . . ."

"You're nuts!" Chris interrupted him. "He did take the gun and he put it in the drawer of his desk. He never had a chance to take the clip. He was called out of the office and then I took the gun back again. It wasn't my gun. I was kind of worried for fear I wouldn't get to send it right back to its owner, you see. You see, a kid loaned me the gun, but it belonged to his father."

I said, "Phil Hannegan did exactly what he should. He didn't want Chris to have an accident with the gun."

"Mrs. Abbott," said Inspector Bradish, "when I want your valuable ideas I'll ask for them. Why did you say you know shorthand?"

"But why write down a lot of lies?"

"Write everything down, Jean," Patrick said. "Chris, the Inspector should have told you that anything you say can be used against you."

"But I didn't do anything, except steal the stamps and the shoebox," Chris said.

"I know you didn't," Patrick said.

Bradish said, with some acid, "This is getting to be very interesting. Hannegan went to Los Angeles, the very day that Leland returned here by way of Los Angeles. Hannegan went to Mexico with Leland. Anybody with eyes can see that Hannegan is that way over Leland's widow."

I looked at Gwen. I had to hand it to her. She could take it.

"Hannegan gets back here on the regular plane a short time before Leland flies in on a special plane. With a woman. For your benefit, Pat, while you were away—on that little vacation you and your wife just now took without my official permission—Mrs. Helen Moore was identified at the morgue as the woman who flew up here with Leland on that special plane. It's all in the family, see? Everybody expected a cut from Leland's dough. But apparently Mrs. Moore knew too much, so she had to go the same way as Leland."

"Philip Hannegan did not see Ernest Leland while in Los Angeles," Nancy said.

"Don't say so, dear," Gwen said. "Don't say anything."

"Go on, Chris," Bradish said.

"There isn't anything else. I never even missed the cartridges . . ."

"Aw, now, Chris! There's a lot of difference in the weight of an empty gun. Yours was fully loaded, of course."

Chris said, "Why, yes, it was. To start with. But . . ."

"It had how many cartridges in it?"

"Why, eight. The clip was full. But I never had that gun out of my pocket from the time I took it from Mr. Hannegan's drawer until—until . . ."

Chris stopped.

Patrick said, "Until you gave it to me, don't you mean, kid?"

"Watch yourself, Pat!" Bradish said.

Patrick said, "The boy came to our place, Sam. He fainted just after he got in, from hunger and exhaustion. The gun was not loaded at that time. I advised Chris to get rid of it, specially since it was not his own gun. Maybe I overdid it. It preyed on his mind until he got up and went out to post it. And was picked up by the police."

Bradish said, with less anger, but carefully avoiding Patrick, "Clips from similar guns are interchangeable, of course. A clip filled with cartridges will slip into any automatic of the same model. This Colt we found in the possession of Chris Leland is one in very common use. Nancy Leland admits that her father owned the Colt automatic. She refers to it now as hers. Maybe Chris's gun is the same vintage. We can check things like that. Nancy says she had no cartridges. We all know they are very hard to get. But Chris's clip fits Nancy's gun, which is why there was one of Chris's fingerprints on the shell of the bullet which murdered Helen Moore. Well, Hannegan slipped the clip out of Chris's gun there in his office and transferred it to Nancy's gun. I'm not saying you saw him do it, Chris."

"For crying out loud!" Gwen snapped.

"What's wrong with that?" Bradish asked. He flinched, however. Gwen got at him, thoroughly. Anybody could see that.

Gwen threw back her taffy-red head.

"You know very little about human nature, Inspector Bradish. You don't understand people. If you did, you would know darn well that Phil Hannegan never did anything of that kind. If he had he would have told you so. He is far too honest and upright for his own good. He gets himself into no end of tangles because he never heard of the five-letter word g-u-i-l-e."

"And you have, Miss Telfer?"

"Darn right I have. You're cockeyed, Inspector Bradish. It's *me* Phil Hannegan is going to marry, for God's sake. You force me to come out with it, and me cherishing it as my pet secret." Gwen pouted. She actually contrived a maidenly blush. "Me—and here I have had to sit, with you calling him her boy friend, and what not! I am ashamed—for you, Inspector. I had a much more lofty notion of our police detectives. I thought you were smart people, and I'm very disappointed indeed."

I looked at Nancy. She did nothing. She just sat, with her long eyes on Gwen.

Bradish moved to the other end of the mantelpiece. He moved away as the heat scorched a leg. He walked across the room. He returned to the fire.

Gwen, sensing her advantage, watched every move he made. She sat stiff and trim as a sail. Her eyes were shining. She was in her element. She was happy.

"I don't want to tell the police how to behave," she went on, her voice now so nicely poised that even Bradish could not take offense, "but I wish you would be more patient. For example, you made one blunder about that hat, Inspector Bradish, as you will find out when you make another contact with Madame Madeleine. I wish you would take the hat out of this room, by the way. The color clashes." She said then, "Anyone who knew Nancy Leland would know that she never would in this world wear that hat."

Our glances fell upon the hat. It was a darling hat. Its pink was so perfect that it clashed no more than a rose would have clashed, but Bradish suddenly made a slight grimace, as though the hat indeed offended his color sense.

"Please, Inspector Bradish, we are all just as anxious as you are to clear up this mess," Gwen said beseechingly. "I'll help you, myself. I'll stop everything and devote my time to this case. I will be giving my time, Inspector, with some financial sacrifice. I don't care. Nancy and Rufus are my friends and Philip Hannegan is my fiance. People mean more than money, Inspector Bradish."

Bradish looked at her, at Patrick, at the fire. He had momentarily lost control of the situation. It worried him. He shrugged his big shoulders.

His stenographer returned to the room and said something to Bradish alone.

The inspector's eyes again ran angrily around the people in the room.

"Which of you knows what became of Hannegan?" he demanded.

EIGHTEEN

Across the hall from the living room, in the study, Bradish asked us to sit down, and sat down himself at the big businesslike desk which held, among other things, the telephone. Patrick was still waiting for his call from San Diego.

Bradish mopped his forehead.

"That Telfer woman is straight dynamite," he said.

"Undiluted," Patrick agreed.

Bradish groaned. "She's right about one thing. I went off the beam about that hat. That hat is what the story writers call a red herring. We have questioned that milliner again. Now she's not sure." Gwen had certainly tipped Madame Madeleine off pronto. "Her books show two hats of the same kind bought four weeks apart and she says she can't be sure—until she talks with her girls—which hat was bought first. My God, we may have to collect hairs for analysis from everybody in her shop."

His voice had taken its bitter tone. He flung out his well-shaped hands, and muttered, "So what?" His eyes went on sparkling. It was a trick of color and light. It had nothing whatever to do with his moods.

Patrick said, "Miss Telfer stuck her own neck out when she claimed the pink hat as her own, didn't she, Sam?"

"Maybe. What made you run out on me, Pat?"

"I asked you first to send me officially."

"Why? No, wait a minute. We've got to find Hannegan and see what he's up to, first."

"Why not call his house, Sam?"

Philip answered his telephone immediately. Bradish asked him if he was coming back pronto or did he have to be sent for. Philip answered that he was practically on his way. Bradish cradled the receiver and, sitting back in his chair, his shoulders thrust forward, his cheeks pink with annoyance, said, "Okay."

Patrick crossed his long legs.

"I've been holding out on you, Sam."

Bradish looked sarcastic. Patrick went on, speaking quietly, as always.

"Jean and I saw Leland and Helen Moore together in that Mexican dive I told you about on the phone. Legendre's place. We saw them not long before he was murdered."

Bradish looked livid, but Patrick held up a hand.

"Now, wait a minute! We didn't know at the time who they were. Either of them. We noticed them because they didn't look like the kind of people you usually see in that kind of place. Naturally, we didn't know they were going to be murdered. I recognized Leland in the wreck, but I didn't know who he was till you told me there at the Mark. We didn't know who the woman was till she walked into this house with Rufus Moore four hours after you told me who Leland was. Naturally, I suspected her then of some connection with his death. I haven't seen you alone since, until now. We haven't had a chance to discuss it."

"No law against your telling me about seeing her on the telephone," Bradish said. "You've not only been with-holding evidence. You may be responsible for the woman's death."

"I hope not," Patrick said. "And I think not. I believe she had to die. In one way or another Helen Moore was marked for death."

"Why?"

"Because she knew too much. Hannegan's another one to keep an eye on, Sam."

Bradish said, "Oh, he told me that cock-and-bull tale about somebody trying to bump him off down in Mexico . . ."

"It ties in, Sam. And Hannegan will be an innocent victim. Maybe Helen Moore wasn't so innocent. I advise you seriously not to leave Hannegan alone at any time when he returns to this house."

Bradish said, "I'll tell him to stay with the others in the living room. I can't chaperon each one, Pat."

Patrick said, "There's something else. I want you to believe me when I say that I have deliberately withheld the information about Leland and Helen Moore being together in the café on account of Nancy Leland. I've been hoping to catch the real murderer in time to prevent Nancy's being the victim of suspicion and scandal. Now we've got to work fast. The morning papers are going to do their worst over the double murders of Ernest Leland and Helen Moore. She looked like a babe. She was a frustrated movie actress. He had plenty of money and was separated from his young wife. Some of the tabloids will embroider all that in their dirtiest. By the way, did you pick up that fellow Legendre at the Mexican place?"

Bradish nodded. "You'd better be right. I had to send a couple of men I needed here. If they had been here on the job, Hannegan wouldn't have got away."

"He'll be back. By the way, I didn't go to the city morgue to look at Ernest Leland. I went to view a body you've got labeled Miguel Nogales."

Bradish started. "What for?"

"He's a member of a dope ring, isn't he, Sam?"

"Could be. Why?"

"His real name is Marco Jones. Or that's the name he went by where he worked, and at the place where he lived."

"Where did he work?" Bradish asked suspiciously.

"He worked for Legendre," Patrick said. "He was a waiter. He waited on us when we were there and he also had the table where Leland and Mrs. Moore sat. He was an addict, too, wasn't he, Sam?"

Bradish said, "What's that got to do with . . ."

Patrick said quickly, as we heard somebody coming in the front door, "You said his murder tied in with something important, something you would probably have to pass along to the Feds. You referred to the Federal Narcotics Bureau, didn't you, Sam? You thought he was a victim of his own gang, didn't you? They kill members who become addicts, you know. Can't trust them."

There was a short pause.

"We've been watching him a good while," Bradish said then. He lifted his voice. "That you, Mr. Hannegan? Come in here, and explain why you left this house."

Philip Hannegan appeared from the hall.

"Moore went to sleep," he said. "I thought I could leave him safely. I went home to make some telephone calls."

"What kind?"

"I called my lawyer. He'll be here in a few minutes to advise Mrs. Leland."

Bradish said, "I thought Miss Telfer was seeing after Mrs. Leland's counsel?"

"She's not getting anywhere," Philip said.

"Okay," Bradish said. "Go into the living room with the others and don't leave this house again. Don't go anywhere alone till I say so. My sergeant is upstairs keeping an eye on Rufus Moore."

"Sorry," Philip said curtly, and went on across the hall. We heard voices as he opened and closed the door.

"Have you questioned Moore?" Patrick asked Inspector Bradish.

"We gave him the works while you were away. No soap."

"You're sure he was in Los Angeles when Leland was murdered?"

"He says he can prove he was at home all night by telephone calls. We checked on him through his neighbors, as I told you. He came home, put his car in, and left at his usual time the next morning. He says he made a few telephone calls. We will check with the people he says he talked to. Otherwise he's got no alibi because he was alone in the house."

"Sam, Helen Moore came to see me just before she was murdered."

Bradish's jaw dropped. He flushed purple.

Patrick said, "I expected to take her home. But Miss Telfer showed up just then and to avoid her Mrs. Moore slipped out the back way and came over here, just in time to get herself shot, apparently. You see, she remembered us being at the dive. She came to explain being up here with Leland. She says she came with him, though he didn't want it, to persuade him to give Nancy a divorce."

"Why?"

"She said because she wanted Nancy to be happy."

"My God," Bradish sighed.

"She may have had other, more urgent reasons," Patrick said. "She probably lied, to prevent her true reasons from coming to light. She lied about one thing for certain. She said she did not come up here with Leland because she had to hurry to catch a train back home. There is no train to Los Angeles between the time we saw her with Leland until eight o'clock in the morning. That takes twelve hours to L.A. She had to get back by plane."

"She went back by plane," Bradish said. "She was pretty conspicuous, you know. She's been identified already as a woman who picked up a seat on the 3 A.M. plane and then at the last minute didn't show up. She was lucky and picked up another place on the 4 A.M. plane. Nobody seemed to know why she didn't take the first flight. She called herself Mrs. Tom Johnson. Plane seats are mighty scarce. She was lucky."

Patrick's eyes gleamed the green color they take on when he is tremendously excited.

Bradish said, "Hannegan told us about seeing Mrs. Moore at the Los Angeles airport. So we contacted the pilot who flew Leland up here again. He went to the morgue and identified the body as that of the woman he brought here with Leland. Then we checked the passengers returning that same night to L.A. and sure enough there she was."

"Fast work, Sam," Patrick said.

"We're doing all right everywhere but right here in the house," Bradish said.

Patrick leaned forward.

"May I question Rufus Moore, Sam?"

"I talked to him till black in the face. He won't be any good till he sleeps off that dope. He must have got a load of it through his system before we woke him up."

"I'd like to try."

Bradish got up and went into the hall. We heard him talking to his sergeant upstairs. In a few minutes the policeman brought Rufus downstairs.

Rufus Moore looked pale, but composed. His big face was yeasty-white and there were great brown circles around his pale brown and now heavy-lidded eyes. He nodded at us, and sat down in the chair Patrick pulled up for him.

He was dressed in the navy chalkline suit he had worn last evening. His tie was neatly tied, but he needed a shave.

"I asked Inspector Bradish if I could talk with you, Rufus," Patrick said. "Have you any idea who killed Leland and your wife?"

Rufus shook his head, one small shake.

"She was acquainted with Leland before you knew her, wasn't she, Rufus?"

Rufus nodded. One nod.

"Her mother knew him, too, I believe?"

A faint light gleamed in the pale eyes. But briefly.

"Did your mother-in-law move to San Diego before you and Helen were married?" Rufus nodded, and looked bored. Patrick asked, "Why?"

"She wasn't well. The climate is milder there."

"What's wrong with her?"

Rufus moved his shoulders.

"Gwen Telfer made the statement tonight that Helen's mother is a dope addict," Patrick said. Rufus looked instantly blank, but Bradish perked right up. "I've been wondering if she got into the habit from being in the traffic? People sometimes do, you know. They get caught in their own evil."

"Oh, cut it out," Rufus said. "I don't like your insinuations . . ."

"I'm not insinuating. I made an observation and I asked you a fair question, Rufus."

"What's fair about it? She's dying, isn't she? Why drag out the dirt? We told Helen she had a bad heart. That's good enough, isn't it?"

"Sure—unless she was in the business. People who peddle dope also peddle away their right to consideration and privacy."

Rufus spoke thickly. "All right. She is a dope-fiend. Helen did not know it. But that doesn't make her a peddler of the stuff. I don't see the point in airing things like that. Nancy will have to know now, and why should she? Mrs. Bishop is dying. She probably won't last another week."

"Who takes care of her, Rufus?"

"A nurse. Not a trained nurse. A friend of hers who has lived with her a long time."

"They always stay in San Diego?"

"That's Mrs. Bishop's home. They've got a little place down in Old Mexico, not far from Agua Caliente, but they don't get down there very often any more. All of which has absolutely nothing to do with these murders."

Patrick's voice sounded hard as he asked, "Well, what does have to do with the murders, Rufus? What are you keeping back?"

"Nothing," Rufus groaned. Drops of sweat appeared on his white forehead. "I don't know anything. I don't understand any of it . . ."

"You didn't want Nancy to divorce Leland," Patrick said, and his voice was like ice. "You were afraid it would affect your job. You didn't care if she loved him or didn't."

"I admit that," Rufus said. "I was wrong. But I always thought that Ernest Leland was a fine man. I thought that Nancy might feel differently, if she took her time about divorcing him. I wanted her to wait. He didn't want the divorce. He had money to make her comfortable. He wanted her to have everything money can buy. She—we—had had a pretty tough time. Maybe I was wrong. But I've got nothing I can hold against Leland. Nothing that has been said makes me feel differently toward him. He was a swell guy."

Bradish leaned on the desk and asked, "What about your wife's flying up here with Leland last night? Did you know that, Mr. Moore?"

Rufus turned his eyes on the Inspector.

"Where did you get that idea?" he asked.

"It's quite true, Rufus," Patrick said.

Rufus considered it.

"If it's true, she had a good reason," he said.

Well, good for old Rufus, I thought. I glanced at Patrick. I could not tell by his face whether he was glad Rufus had given that answer, or sorry.

The telephone rang. Inspector Bradish took it and handed the phone to Patrick. "Long distance," he said. "You can go in with the others, Mr. Moore," he said to Rufus.

Rufus got up heavily, like an old man, and slowly left the room.

NINETEEN

I sat watching Inspector Bradish watching Pat as he took the telephone call. The official ears fairly reached out for anything they might pick up. They got nothing, and disappointment took some of the dazzle out of those blue eyes.

Patrick said, "Yes, Johnny . . . nice work . . . Fast, too . . . Oh, I see. . . . Two nice motherly old ladies active in church and community work. . . . I see. Mrs. Bishop is now bedridden but her friend Miss Copeland carries on with the help of a temporary nurse. . . . Cancer, you say? Oh, I see . . . Yep, they sometimes get to be addicts in cases like that . . . Miss Copeland went down to their place across the border yesterday? Plump, middle-aged, gray hair, printed rayon dress . . . What kind of car? I see. . . ."

They talked on. Patrick said then for Johnny to call him if he picked up anything else and to send him his bill. But before hanging up he pressed down the receiver hook gently with his thumb and released it with the receiver against his ear.

He cradled it. "Anybody upstairs?" he asked Bradish.

"Nope. Not now."

"Where's the other phone?"

"Right where it was, right where Mrs. Moore herself put it last night. I didn't want anything in that room touched till I could go over it myself. Why?"

Patrick said, "I wanted to be sure no one listened in. I would suggest that you get in touch with the proper people and have a certain Miss Copeland stopped at the Tiajuana customs house when she comes in from Mexico tomorrow morning. I don't know, but I shouldn't wonder if she has some hidden compartments built into her Ford car. For smuggling in opium. She's a motherly old girl of fifty-odd in the usual print dress and the usual dowdy hat, I'm told, and since she goes in and out of the country pretty regularly she will be well acquainted with the customs men."

"On what authority am I to do this?" Bradish asked, elaborately.

"None. Just on another of my hunches, Sam. John Grace tells me that Mrs. Bishop is supposed to be dying of cancer. She takes morphine, however, presumably to ease the pain. Grace went straight to the temporary nurse who is looking after her and reported what she said. We may get something more authentic later but what we've got's enough to go on."

Bradish still objected.

"It's no joke, asking what you want, Pat."

"Be pretty nice to get credit for the tip-off, Sam. If it's okay. It's all yours, if you want it."

"I don't want it," Bradish said.

But he picked up the phone and called somebody at the Federal Bureau of Narcotics and passed along the tip. "For what it's worth," he groused.

"Now, let's talk to Nancy Leland," Patrick said.

"It's no use," Bradish objected. "Same with that Chinese woman. Not one word she said made any sense."

"Do you mind if I talk to Nancy?"

Bradish consulted his watch.

"In my presence, then, Pat. And for not more than five minutes."

Patrick nodded. Bradish stepped across the hall. When he returned both Nancy Leland and Gwendolyn Telfer came with him. Gwen announced straight off that she had not yet got in touch with her lawyer and that Nancy was to say nothing till she did.

"That's all right, Gwen," Patrick said. "You know I have Nancy's interests at heart. Suppose you run along and leave the interview to me, please."

"I'll do nothing of the kind, Pat."

"Scram!" Patrick said. But Gwen looked around for a place to seat herself.

With one lithe movement Patrick moved in on her, picked her up, and set her outside. "Now, go back where you belong before we turn *you* over to the police," he said.

He shut the door. Nancy was sitting on the edge of a chair which Sam Bradish had held for her.

Patrick said, "Nancy, where was Rosalie Wong last night at the time Ernest Leland was killed?"

"I suppose she was at home," Nancy said. "Her own home."

"She went to a party, you said?"

"Yes. She usually spent the night in Chinatown, with her sisters, when she went to any sort of affair. The Chinese keep late hours, you know, but her mother didn't like her coming up here very late when alone."

Patrick asked, "Did she wear your pink hat to the party?"

Nancy looked blank.

Patrick said, "You didn't like that hat. You never wanted it. Gwen forced it on you because she thinks you dress too plainly. But Rosalie was crazy about the hat and you knew it would give her a big kick to wear it to her party so you let her wear it, but you didn't actually give it to her—though you meant to later on—because you knew that Gwen would clamp down on you if you gave it away, and she found out about it. You're afraid of Gwen."

"I'm not afraid of Gwen," Nancy said. "But she does make such a row if you don't do everything just the way she likes that—well, maybe you kind of evade. How did you know what you just said? Are you a mind-reader?"

Patrick smiled. "Nope. I just tried to put myself in your place, Nancy. That hair found in the hat will very likely turn out to be Rosalie Wong's. She'd had a permanent, hadn't she?"

Nancy did not answer. Bradish sat forward in his chair, visibly holding back from chiming in.

"You will help no one," Patrick said, "by trying to protect Rosalie. The police will only call it withholding evidence and it will make you an accessory. Rosalie did not murder Ernest Leland, but there is the hat, and perhaps the hair will make it seem more her hat than yours, now, to the police. She's a lovely-looking girl. The police will draw the obvious conclusion."

Nancy said nothing. Her face was white again, and a complete mask.

Inspector Bradish cut in.

"See here, Mrs. Leland, was your former husband mixed up with that Chinese girl? Is that why you left him?"

Nancy said indignantly, "Of course he wasn't! I told you I left him because we were uncongenial. That's the truth."

"But you lend the girl your hat and it's in the car when we find him murdered. How come?" Nancy was silent. "And you say she wasn't expected home that night?" No reply. "Did she come home, or didn't she?"

"She didn't," Nancy said. "You questioned her mother about that. Mary Wong told you the truth. Rosalie can certainly prove that she spent the night with her sisters."

"Then what about that hat?"

Nancy was again silent, and Bradish said, acidly, "That hat will convict you, Mrs. Leland. That friend of yours, Miss Gwen Telfer, thinks that policemen are dumb, and evidently she thinks they're color-blind, too, if she's got the notion they can't tell a pink from a blue hat."

Nancy put her hands together. They kept twisting.

"What was Rosalie Wong to Ernest Leland?" Bradish demanded.

"Oh, you make me sick," Nancy said.

Patrick spoke up. "I don't think Leland's vice was women, Sam. We discussed that, remember? His trouble was greed. Avarice. Whatever you want to call it. It's not a very nice vice. I'll take a drunk or a woman-chaser any day myself."

"Let's stick to the hat," said Bradish.

"I know nothing about the hat that you don't know already," Nancy said. "I don't know how you dreamed up the idea I gave it to Rosalie Wong."

"That's all, Nancy," Patrick said. "You can go back with the others, if Inspector Bradish agrees."

Inspector Bradish didn't agree. He kept her five minutes longer and he hammered her with questions and insinuations and she remained entirely dumb.

Then she was allowed to return to the living room.

Bradish took out his handkerchief and wiped his face.

"You can't hang the woman because her hat was in that car. It's not enough. You know a thing, but proving it is something else. She's beautiful, in a way, too. She can win over any jury. She almost has me mesmerized, Pat. So help me, I admire a woman with guts. But Hannegan will be easier to get at. If he's her boy-friend." The word boy-friend meant more than it usually does the way he put it. "We'll work on him some more," Bradish said.

"Waste of time," Patrick said.

Bradish shrugged. "Okay, Superman," said he, "then why does Mrs. Nancy Leland freeze up like that every time she's questioned?"

"Because she thinks she knows who killed her husband."

"You're darned right she knows. She did it herself. Maybe with Hannegan's help, though. That tall tale he told about what happened in Mexico just makes him that more suspicious. She stuck the hypo into Leland and polished off her sister-in-law with the Colt automatic, because Helen Moore knew she killed Leland."

Patrick said, "You've searched the house thoroughly for the gun?"

"We have not! We haven't searched the living room or the room where Helen Moore was to sleep. I stopped the men when Chris Leland was picked up trying to get rid of his gun. Then you had that bright idea about Legendre and—if that's funny business, Pat . . ."

"Try the kitchen?"

"That's one place that got the works. Pat, we're wasting time. I've got to talk to Hannegan, right now."

"May I search the kitchen again, Sam?"

Bradish was again suspicious. "I'll go with you," he said.

We walked along the hall and entered the service hall through the door under the staircase. In the kitchen Mary Wong, in a white overall, rose from a straight chair.

"I told you you could go to bed," Bradish said.

She made her funny little bow.

"I could not sleep. Breakfast will soon be needed, or tea and coffee."

I glanced at the kitchen clock. It was five minutes to four.

"We've come to search the kitchen again for the gun which killed Mrs. Moore, Mary," Patrick said. He crossed directly to a flour bin, one of the big old-fashioned kind built under a built-in table. He then pulled open a drawer, found a long fork, and poked this carefully into what looked like a lot of flour. It struck metal!

He had the gun out of the flour pronto, protecting it with a clean linen dish-towel.

"Very neat," Bradish snapped. "Too neat. How come?"

"Never mind that now," Patrick said. "Why did you hide it, Mary?"

Bradish's eyes stuck out.

Mary Wong was silent.

The little woman stood perfectly still. Her hands were linked in front of her flat stomach. Against the white uniform they looked small and yellow.

"I notice the safety catch is on," Patrick said. "I can see that you know how to handle a gun, Mary. I suppose that Mr. Moore, being helpless, was always apprehensive of being done bodily harm. I know he had Nancy learn to use a gun. And you too, of course."

It was a statement. Only a slight narrowing of Mary's slanting sloe-black eyes seemed to confirm it.

Patrick said, "You took the clip from Chris Leland's automatic. You slipped it into this one."

"No," Mary said.

"You took the clip," Patrick said, in the same low even authentic voice. Mary was silent now. "Chris came to see Nancy Leland. You took his raincoat and asked him to wait in the living room. The coat was heavy. You looked in the pockets and found the gun. It was the same model as Nancy Leland's. You slipped out the clip and transferred it to her gun. You wiped the fingerprints off the clip, but the cartridges had been inserted by Chris Leland, which is why one of his prints was on the shell we found beside Mrs. Moore's dead body."

Mary spoke flatly, but still with her tremendous dignity.

"I don't know how you think up all that, Mr. Abbott. But it is true that I took the clip, as you call it, out of his gun. I was frightened. The boy seemed so angry. I was afraid he would harm Miss Nancy."

Bradish moved in. "You shot Mrs. Moore!" he declared.

Mary Wong's glance stabbed him like a knife. She made no answer. "Your girl wore the hat," he accused. "She was in that car with Leland!" His sparkling eyes stabbed her in return.

"No," Mary said.

"Where was the gun kept?" Patrick asked.

"In the room they call the study," Mary said. "In a drawer in the big desk where the telephone stands."

"You have a telephone extension in your rooms, haven't you, Mary?"

"Yes, sir. It's old-fashioned. So they did not take it for the war."

"Did you listen in when Mr. Leland called Mrs. Leland? A short time before he was murdered just outside this house?"

"I was not at home at that time, Mr. Abbott."

"You'll have to prove that to the satisfaction of the police," Bradish said.

Mary ignored him completely.

Patrick asked, softly, "Why have you been following me everywhere I go, Mary?"

Again the eyes narrowed. There was no reply.

"We're wasting time," Bradish said. "There's no use holding out on us any longer, Mary. We've got the hat. The hat has a hair in it which we can prove is one of your girl's. We've probably got her in jail by this time. We work fast. Okay, come out with it. Had Leland been playing around with the girl?"

The yellow hands were twisting. In spite of a frantic effort of will the palms kept rubbing against each other.

"That is not true," Mary said.

"My God!" Bradish said. "Of course it's true. You did the whole thing. You know how to use a hypo, of course. You helped nurse Nancy Leland's father. It wasn't any trouble for a Chinese to get the cyanide. You Chinese can always find a way."

Mary darted him another deadly look. The hands were again quiet. It was only when Rosalie was attacked that she grew weak. Poor thing. Poor, poor little thing.

"Here, Sam," Patrick said, handing over the gun, wrapped in the towel. "Let's take Mary into the living room. We might just as well get this thing over and done with, don't you agree? The jig's up. Everything is clear now."

"They're all in it," Bradish said. "I've said so all the time. Good God Almighty!"

TWENTY

Gloom and depression hung like crepe over the group in the living room. The fire had died down to a heap of coals which were slowly going out. Rufus Moore sat in the corner of one of the sofas. His head drooped on his chest. His bulging eyes were closed. Their lashes lay on his pale cheeks, giving him a vulnerable look. I felt sorry for him, too. He was sad.

Nancy was sitting where we had left her, and she looked as if her nerve had deserted her. Even Gwen Telfer seemed somewhat deflated. Chris Leland slept, curled up in a chair in the background. Philip Hannegan was pacing the room. He came to a halt and consulted his watch as we entered. The police stenographer rose from his table when he saw his superior.

Nancy stirred with alarm when Mary Wong was ushered in. She started to speak, but a low word from Philip stopped her.

Patrick said, taking his stand near the fireplace, "Mary has been concealing evidence to protect you, Nancy. We know now that she took the cartridges from Chris's gun. It was sheer chance that the clip fits yours, but, after all not miraculous, because the model is one in very common use. You kept this gun in a drawer in the study. When Leland called you in the middle of the night you thought of the gun. You may have answered the phone downstairs and, automatically, you opened the table drawer where the gun lay, and there, as if by magic, lay the clip which Mary Wong had removed from Chris Leland's gun. You slipped it into your gun."

Nancy fell for it apparently.

"Suppose I did?" she said. She was not convincing. "Well, I'll admit now that I was afraid of him. He terrified me. He was so cold and calculating. All right? So what? But I didn't answer the phone downstairs. I had one beside my bed."

"Leland wasn't shot," Patrick reiterated. "He was killed with cyanide. Anybody who wants it enough can get cyanide. But those fine hypos which you used to give your father injections are now extremely hard to get. They're swell, of course. They don't hurt at all. The victim hardly knows when he's stuck."

Nancy's face looked gray with fear. Her eyes seemed stretched and depthless.

"It's no use," Patrick told her gently. "I know you think you are shielding Mary Wong and Rosalie because you aren't being entirely open with us about lending Rosalie the pink hat . . ."

Gwen exploded.

"Mary and Rosalie? Do you mean to tell me, Nancy, that you've let me get all hot and bothered just to protect a couple of Chinks? Did you pretend to play ball with me the way you did just to give *them* a break?"

"I'm not finished yet," Patrick said to Gwen. Inspector Bradish had not yet spoken. He was standing in the shadows a little away from the crowd. He had put a cigarette between his lips but had not yet given it a light. He was watching Patrick with keen but very suspicious attention. Patrick said, "Helen Moore came to see me tonight, Nancy." Rufus Moore opened his drowsy eyes, alert for the first time to the new direction the affair was taking. "She came to tell me that she had come here from Los Angeles the other night with Ernest Leland. It was no longer a secret, but I don't think she knew that yet. She said she came along just to try to persuade Ernest to give you an uncontested divorce. She said she wanted you to be happy. That was all she wanted, she said, and that was why she had come. She herself was happily married, she said, and she knew it meant much more than a lot of money."

Tears shone in Nancy's eyes. She let them drift down her cheeks, stoically choosing to ignore them.

Rufus dropped his eyelids. He was the one it was hardest for, after all.

"Having got Leland's promise, Helen went back to Los Angeles," Patrick said. "She told me she took the one o'clock train. She lied."

Rufus stiffened and looked mad. The gray look came back in Nancy's face.

"There is no one o'clock train to Los Angeles," Patrick said. "There was none she could get before eight o'clock in the morning. That takes twelve hours. It couldn't've got her home in time to return here with Rufus as soon as Leland was identified as the murdered man. She went back by plane. She booked a seat on the three A.M. plane. Although she was in the airport when the plane took off she did not claim her seat. She was lucky and picked up another seat on the four o'clock flight.

The murderer of Ernest Leland used the place on the three o'clock plane his wife failed to claim."

One afternoon two weeks later we bought Inspector Sam Bradish a drink at the Mark.

The prospect had been a fine evening when we made the date. But before it came off the fog rolled in, and here we sat, high in the sky, at one of the tables with banquettes upholstered in pale-pink leather, and with our view precisely rimmed by the plate-glass windows. Clouds swirled in white silence around the glass-enclosed room and there was no outlook at all.

Patrick loved the weather. I tried to.

Bradish was looking successful.

"I guess we've rounded up all of them, Pat. All that matter. Biggest haul in narcotics on record. Half a million dollars worth of pure opium in sealed cans was cached in what they called the Coast depot alone."

"You've done it with the minimum of publicity, Sam."

"You have to, Pat."

"Well, the secrecy has been fine for Nancy Leland."

"It wasn't sentiment, Pat. We needed secrecy to cover what we had to do."

Bradish sipped his bourbon. I had finished my Manhattan and, after a couple of glances at the fog, was wishing I had a second.

"Some racket!" Bradish said. "Ernest K. Leland put up the capital and supervised the whole gang. The only people who knew he was the works were Rufus Moore, Legendre, and Helen Moore's mother, Mrs. Bishop. Legendre sang, as he would, and Mrs. Bishop made a voluntary statement when she learned that Helen was dead. She had got into the traffic for Helen's sake. She and Ernest Leland roped Rufus Moore into it for the same reason. Helen herself was never actively in it, though financed by it. But Rufus always suspected her, just the same. Mrs. Bishop thought if she bought her daughter fine clothes and gave her money to spend she'd get to be a star. Rufus kept it up because he thought in that way he could hold her. He was wild about her."

"How was it done, exactly?" I asked Inspector Bradish. I had heard Pat's story, but wanted the police version.

"The opium poppies were grown in Mexico expressly for the gang. The dope was transported by Indians on foot or by donkeys over the mountains until finally it arrived at the seaside cottage where Mrs. Bishop and her companion Miss Copeland went for week-ends, once or twice a month. Two nice motherly old girls like that excited no suspicion when they crossed the border. They got acquainted with the customs men, and

I suppose they were hardly ever inspected at all. We found very ingenious secret compartments built into the gasoline tank of their Ford car." Bradish frowned. "The funny thing is that Leland would get mixed up in it. He already had more dough than he could use."

"Avarice," Patrick reminded him. "Greed. The lust to possess, even at such cost in human degradation."

Bradish shuddered.

"It's horrible. If he knew as much about addicts as you get to know on the force he wouldn't've touched the traffic with a pole."

"*He* would have," Patrick said. "He was that kind. His character has fascinated me all through this business. He was what I'd call pure unadulterated evil, Sam."

I said, "That reminds me of something Nancy Leland said to Gwen Telfer. Except it was the very opposite. She said that Mary Wong was pure undefiled goodness."

"She is a good woman," said Bradish. "She was only being loyal to Nancy and Rufus Moore in keeping silent. That's second nature in the Chinese. What gripes me is Moore's polishing himself off with that morphine. He was dying all the time! If we had suspected that his drowsiness came from morphine instead of those sleeping pills we might have kept him alive."

"Not after the amount he'd injected," Patrick said.

"It's tricky stuff, Pat. Sometimes they're a long time going under. Hours. They'll get bright as dollars sometimes. Then pop off suddenly, and forever."

Patrick signaled for another round of drinks.

The fog was turning bluish, with the fading of the day. It sank me.

"Where did he get the morphine?" I asked.

Bradish chuckled. "He said from a supply a doctor prescribed for his mother-in-law. He'd've had no trouble getting it, I guess. He carried it, like the cyanide, to kill himself with if caught."

Patrick said, "Leland had an ideal set-up for his racket, Sam. He was all mixed up in defense projects, both here and in Mexico. The Mexicans had even given him a diplomatic pass. He could flit back and forth as easy as pie. Keep an eye on the production end of his opium racket in Mexico and on the distribution here. Everything was jake. But they always make a mistake. His was involving Rufus Moore. Rufus was a bad risk. He was too sentimental."

"How come Leland went to that dive?" I asked.

Bradish answered. "The waiter, Marco, was supposed to meet him in Portsmouth Square for a message for Legendre. Marco was dopey and forgot to go. So Leland went to the dive. His purpose was merely to let

Legendre know he was in town. Legendre's move was to phone Leland as soon as he could do so privately. It was urgent to get word to the old ladies in San Diego that there was a load of the stuff arriving at the bungalow near Tiajuana, or Leland wouldn't've risked going to the dive. That's why Marco got bumped off. He failed to keep his date with Leland. He had become an addict. Once that happens, the gang kills them."

"Rufus didn't kill him, too?" I asked.

"We don't know exactly who killed Marco but it wasn't Rufus Moore," Bradish said. "We'll get Legendre on that count eventually. But we haven't yet trapped him into an admission that the gang popped off Marco Jones."

"It's very complicated," I said.

"Very," Bradish said. The drinks came. He picked up his and held it up without saying anything, and after taking a sip, said, "Pat, I owe you an apology. But you sure did get in my hair."

"I was trying to spare Nancy Leland some very nasty newspaper space."

"You ought to have told me right at first, though, that you saw Leland and Mrs. Moore in that dive."

"A good Marine never lets the rules hamper him while getting a situation well in hand, Sam."

Bradish smiled, but only out of politeness.

"I didn't get it. I figured you were cooking up schemes to get yourself in on the dough."

"He wouldn't take one penny!" I said. The Scot in me resented this slightly, too.

Bradish said, "And right in the middle you had to go and run out on me like that! As if there wasn't enough trouble already!"

"Well, since my hunch about Marco Jones and our friend Legendre clicked . . ."

"It's a darn good thing for you it did, Pat!"

"Oh, it would, Inspector Bradish," I said.

The Inspector smiled again, but only politely.

"How come you got that hunch, Pat?"

"I went back to the dive twice that night. The first time was right after Helen Moore came to see me at our apartment. Gwen Telfer turned up in a cab just then and I used it to go down to the dive. I wanted to see if the waiter remembered Helen's coming there with Ernest Leland. She had lied to me about taking a train—I happen to know train schedules fairly well—so I suspected her then of knowing more about Leland's death than she admitted. The headwaiter told me that Marco wasn't there. His attitude was peculiar. You had said something about a corpse in the morgue that excited my curiosity, so I dashed over and had a look myself. It was Marco. While I was at headquarters the message came in that a woman had been murdered at Nancy Leland's address. I was pretty scared. I was afraid it was Nancy."

"What made you guess that Marco was suspected of being part of a dope ring? I certainly didn't spill that, Pat."

"You said he was mixed up in something you would have to pass along to the Feds. I guessed you might mean narcotics. It's common knowledge that Mexico is the chief source of illicit drugs now that Japan is using her huge traffic to demoralize the Chinese. Then Phil Hannegan had almost got bumped off down in Mexico. He thought it was because Leland had it in for him. He didn't like him and he thought the feeling was returned. But Leland's type wouldn't have given a damn if Phil liked him or not. Leland got scared, because of Phil's attitude, that he had happened onto some knowledge of his connection with the drug traffic. When Phil flew home without joining him in Mexico he got in a dither. That was why he wouldn't wait for a regular flight in Los Angeles. That was why he took the risk of going directly to the dive, so that Legendre would know he was there and would get in touch with him at once. But he had the bad luck to meet up with Helen Moore."

"And she came along, so he got murdered," Bradish said. "And so did she. And Rufus Moore too is dead."

"Rufus went out to the Los Angeles airport to pick up their car," Patrick said. "He told us that before he passed out. He got there just in time to see Helen getting into the private plane with Ernest Leland. He was frantic with jealousy, and suspicion. He drove the car home, mulling it over in his methodic way. He put the car in, went into the house. That's what the neighbors truthfully reported. There is a plane every hour now from Los Angeles to San Francisco during the evening. (We were lucky to get his full statement, Sam.) Rufus left home soon after arriving there and went back to the airport. Under an assumed name he got a seat for San Francisco. He arrived here shortly after midnight. He called Leland's hotel and was told that he was out of town. By that time he was desperate. But he went home, that is to Nancy's—a natural thing for him to do under the circumstances, thinking he would go to bed and have it out with Leland next day. He had always kept his key. He let himself in. The telephone started ringing. He hurried along to the study. Nancy answered it upstairs before he got to the phone in the study, but he took down the receiver and heard Leland insisting on seeing her and asking for an immediate divorce. He imagined that Leland was doing it to marry Helen. After Nancy hung up Rufus hung up. You remember, Jean, that she said there seemed to be somebody listening in.

"Rufus knew that the revolver was in the drawer of the desk where the phone stood. He opened the drawer. There lay the gun, and beside it the clip Mary had removed from Chris's gun. It was Rufus who put the clip into the automatic. He handled it with gloves. As your ballistics boys reported later, there were no fingerprints save that one of Chris Leland's which was found on the shell I picked up next Helen Moore's dead body.

"Then Rufus had a better idea. Ever since getting hooked up with the dope racket, Rufus had carried a hypo of cyanide, meaning to kill himself if he was ever caught. Cyanide is quiet. He slipped out and waited behind the hedge for Leland to arrive. When he came, Mary Wong was in the car. She got out and went directly up the drive to the service entrance. Rufus stepped out and murdered Leland before he got out of the car. But Mary had forgotten the hat in the car. Nancy had lent Rosalie the hat, and her mother was bringing it home when Leland happened to see her walking along Powell Street. He gave her a lift. He always made it a point to be civil to the Wongs, in case he might need them. Inside the house Mary remembered the hat. She returned for it and her sharp eyes recognized Rufus Moore as he got into the car and started down the hill. She thought he was moving it for better parking. She followed on foot. She wanted the hat. At the intersection, as we know, he stepped out and let the car roll. Rufus left Russian Hill by way of the steep steps between Green and Taylor Streets. Mary heard the car crash and ran down the hill till she saw us coming up just below the fog line. She still wanted the hat but she turned and ran back, because she didn't want to give evidence against Rufus. She didn't know then that Leland was murdered. She did know that Rufus, for some reason, had deliberately wrecked the car. And she kept following us around afterwards, trying to make up her mind to tell me that she knew that Rufus had killed Ernest Leland."

Bradish said, "Rufus never knew that Mary saw him take the car."

"Nope."

I said, "When did he inject the morphine? In himself?"

"Right after he shot his wife," Bradish said.

I said, "Do you mean he was already under its influence when he slipped out of Nancy's house? After Phil Hannegan left him asleep—as he thought—and slipped out himself to go home to call a lawyer for Nancy? You mean Rufus was already doped when he sneaked on over to our place and bashed in Pat's head with a wrench he picked up in Nancy's garage?"

"He sure was," Bradish said. "It's funny stuff, Mrs. Abbott. Moore got it into his head that if Pat was dead no one would ever know the truth about the dope. Rufus would rather have had people think he killed

Leland and his wife and himself for jealousy. He could still think of Nancy and he thought the disgrace of his peddling dope would be visited on her. Some guard I had around that house! Gosh! Also you oughtn't've had your door unlocked." Bradish paused, to breathe. "I must say Hannegan had me bothered. I wasn't sure he wasn't mixed up in the deal himself."

"Phil thought Gwen Telfer had done it," I said.

"She had me bothered, too," Bradish said.

I said, "She came to our place after having got out of that taxi, after wandering around in the mist. Her coat wasn't even wet."

"She had reversed it. The tweed side was damp," Patrick said. "She was just keeping an eye on Phil, and getting some excitement."

"She's a busybody," Bradish said.

Patrick nodded. "Phil stood for Gwen's antics because he thought that with enough rope she would hang herself," he said.

"And Nancy because she was shielding Rosalie and Mary Wong," I said.

"If people wouldn't be so loyal to each other solving murders would be easier," said Bradish. "Smart of you to trap Rufus into a confession the way you did, Patrick."

"Thanks, Sam. I knew when you said that Helen Moore had passed up a seat in the three o'clock plane, when she was right in the airport, that there must have been somebody in the airport she wished to avoid. She was desperately anxious to get back to Los Angeles and she couldn't be at all sure of another seat. I didn't know Rufus was the man she was trying to avoid. I guessed it. I accused him, and he confessed."

I said, "Did Rufus learn that Helen had seen him at the airport?"

"Yes. She had told him. She told us she hadn't, but she was afraid he had seen her, so she told him about coming here with Leland."

"So that's really why he shot her and then killed himself."

"Yes. He watched her. He went crazy when she slipped out of the house. He got the gun and waited for her. Afterwards he shot himself full of morphine."

"Was she threatening Leland with exposure when he saw them at the dive? If he wouldn't divorce Nancy?"

"Yes. That was what she said she would not tell us. She would not have exposed his racket, but she was afraid that everything would come out if stubborn Nancy started to fight."

In the dusk the fog around us had turned gray. The dim lighting, designed to emphasize the brilliant nightscape when it was clear, gave the people at the tables about us an eerie look. I got interested in an oldish man and a young gal at the table next to ours. I could see them reflected in the window.

"That Telfer woman was one long pain," said Bradish.

"Crazy about business," Pat said, grinning. "What happens to the money?"

"There's plenty, even after fines are paid and taxes deducted. I guess Telfer was just worried about her bread and butter, if you can call thirty grand a year such."

"She wanted Hannegan. In her fashion," Patrick said.

"She got over it fast."

"Sure. Just as soon as she was given the go-ahead again on the Leland advertising accounts, she was okay. I talked Nancy into taking her inheritance and divvying it with Chris. They're both good people. Good people ought to take money that comes their way. They use it for the benefit of other people."

"Yeah," Bradish said. "She'll marry Hannegan."

"Yeah. Good pair, Sam."

"Yep."

I was watching that couple, in the glass. The man was pleading, as if for his life. The gal was a hard young thing. He didn't make a dent.

Patrick and Inspector Bradish talked about the money, until Bradish said, "The smartest thing you did was know where that gun was."

"Elementary, Sam. I couldn't miss it."

"Says you."

"I mean it. When we walked into the hall where Helen Moore lay dead Mary was standing to the left of the body. There was that thin white line on the front of her black dress. It might have come from the edge of an old-fashioned flour bin. And it had. She had hidden the gun, as we know. Out of loyalty."

The awful thing was that I myself had seen that white line. I had thought it a ray of light. My goodness!

And how depressing. It was a clue. It was the kind of clue that even I should have got. And I'd missed it.

I glanced at the fog. It had darkened. It seemed a blackish menace from which we were spared by the delicate barrier of the dully shining windows. I caught then a slight movement at the next table. The man had covered his eyes suddenly with one hand. He looked as if he would like to cry. The girl sat tight. Now what? Oh, what a town! What a terrible, wonderful, gay, depressing, thrilling, miserable, delightful place was San Francisco! "Darn that hat!" Bradish was saying, when I listened again, and Patrick was signaling the waiter to bring us more drinks.

THE END

About the Rue Morgue Press

"Rue Morgue Press is the old-mystery lover's best friend, reprinting high quality books from the 1930s and '40s."
—*Ellery Queen's Mystery Magazine*

Since 1997, the Rue Morgue Press has reprinted scores of traditional mysteries, the kind of books that were the hallmark of the Golden Age of detective fiction. Authors reprinted or to be reprinted by the Rue Morgue include Catherine Aird, Delano Ames, H. C. Bailey, Morris Bishop, Nicholas Blake, Dorothy Bowers, Pamela Branch, Joanna Cannan, John Dickson Carr, Glyn Carr, Torrey Chanslor, Clyde B. Clason, Joan Coggin, Manning Coles, Lucy Cores, Frances Crane, Norbert Davis, Elizabeth Dean, Carter Dickson, Eilis Dillon, Michael Gilbert, Constance & Gwenyth Little, Marlys Millhiser, Gladys Mitchell, Patricia Moyes, James Norman, Stuart Palmer, Craig Rice, Kelley Roos, Charlotte Murray Russell, Maureen Sarsfield, Margaret Scherf, Juanita Sheridan and Colin Watson..

To suggest titles or to receive a catalog of Rue Morgue Press books write 87 Lone Tree Lane, Lyons, CO 80540, telephone 800-699-6214, or check out our website, www.ruemorguepress.com, which lists complete descriptions of all of our titles, along with lengthy biographies of our writers.